ALSO

The Betrayal
The Return
The Wanderer

Highland Vow

American Hearts Romances
Secret Hearts
Runaway Hearts
Forbidden Hearts

For more information, visit jljarvis.com.

THE CHRISTMAS TREE INN

THE CHRISTMAS TREE INN

A HOLIDAY HOUSE NOVEL

J.L. JARVIS

THE CHRISTMAS TREE INN
A Holiday House Novel

Published by Bookbinder Press
bookbinderpress.com

ISBN 978-1-942767-22-0 (trade paperback)
ISBN 978-1-942767-19-0 (paperback)
ISBN 978-1-942767-18-3 (ebook)

ONE

"I need something sharper." Molly searched the kitchen table, strewn with rubber stamps, pens, and paper scraps.

Dakota pointed at Molly's glass. "Take it easy on those. You're looking a little violent."

Molly tossed her head back and laughed. "I know. Diet soda does that to me. Be right back." While Dakota worked on her homemade Christmas cards, Molly went to the front desk of the inn to search for some scissors. The last time she'd seen them, they were there, so she crouched down and rummaged through shelves and drawers, determined to find them.

"Aha!" Molly leapt to her feet, wielding the scissors. "Oh!" She stared, wide-eyed.

Before her stood a tall, good-looking man in a suit so perfectly fitted that he appeared to have just stepped out of an ad in a men's magazine. He looked almost too good to be real, except for the furrowed eyebrows. "If you're going to attack me, the blade end might be more effective."

Molly's jaw dropped, and she lowered the scissors. "I'm so sorry. I didn't hear you come in. I was just looking for these."

His mouth quirked at the corner. "And you found them."

Molly met his enthralling brown eyes with a squint. "Yes. Sorry." She set the scissors down on a shelf beneath the counter. "So. Welcome to the Christmas Tree Inn. May I help you?" She gazed at his light-brown hair and marveled at how perfect it was—neat and trimmed, every strand in place. As the silence between them stretched out, the front door swung open.

In strode a willowy blond woman with the limbs of a gazelle minus the grace. She accessorized her designer apparel with a faint air of boredom that promised the effervescence of a fashion runway model. With a look of disdain, she glanced up from her phone. "Still checking in?"

Molly came to her senses and got back to work, scanning the reservations listed on the computer screen. "You must be Mr. Moreton? And..." She smiled. "Ms. Pomeroy?"

Ms. Pomeroy condescended to sigh, which Molly took as a confirmation.

Molly nodded and forced a cordial smile at the woman, who looked only slightly older than she was, perhaps in her midtwenties. For such a young woman, she had an impressive perception of her place in the world. Molly multitasked, checking them in while she tallied the days before they would check out. Sensing eyes on her, she turned to Mr. Zachary Moreton. His gaze rendered her slightly off-balance, but the unexpected warmth in his eyes drew her to him. His expression was probably not any kinder than anyone else's, but it proved such a stark contrast to his girlfriend's that Molly found it reassuring. She retrieved a room key from a drawer and handed it to him.

"How quaint," Ms. Pomeroy said as she slowly inspected the room. It might have passed for a compliment if she hadn't said it with such a weary look on her face. With no warning, Penelope Pomeroy turned and headed upstairs.

Molly rushed after her. "I'll show you to your—" But the woman was already nearing the top. Molly glanced back at Mr. Moreton, who seemed in no rush to catch up.

"We'll be fine." With an apologetic smile, Zachary Moreton thanked her and headed upstairs.

Molly called after him. "It's the second room on the left."

"Thank you."

She watched him for a moment longer than necessary then realized what she was doing. Admiring guests' athletic physiques as they climbed flights of stairs to their rooms was utterly inappropriate. Still, the guy clearly worked out. Molly shook her head. *Stop it.* She walked to the reception area and found Dakota leaning on the kitchen door, arms folded.

"Who's your friend?"

"Who, the new guest?" Molly found him attractive, but she couldn't admit it. She tried to maintain an aura of professionalism. "He's not really my type." She thanked God she was not under oath.

"Oh, really?" Dakota wasn't buying it. "What's wrong with him? Name one flaw."

Molly's expression was the same one she made when encountering beets. "Too handsome. You can't trust a guy who looks like he's stepped out of a cuff link ad."

Dakota folded her arms. "That's a bit looks-ist of you."

"Right. Because the impossibly gorgeous are such a poor, downtrodden lot."

"What if he turned out to like you?" Dakota's eyes twinkled.

Molly let out an exaggerated sigh. "I'd do my best to let him down easy."

Dakota raised an eyebrow. "He could let me down easy, if you know what I mean."

Molly turned Dakota around by the shoulders and nudged her toward the kitchen. "Leave the new guest alone."

"Guest? You mean your new boyfriend." Dakota practically sang it.

"And his girlfriend?" Molly sat down then realized she'd left the scissors at the front desk and went to retrieve them. When she returned moments later, Dakota was waiting, chin on hands.

"So, what's his name? Where's he from? When's the wedding date?"

"Whose?"

"Yours. Or mine, if you don't want him." Dakota's eyes glazed over. "June weddings are so pedestrian. And why wait? A small wedding in March...or April. In Paris. The bridesmaids could all wear berets."

"And the groomsmen could all dress like mimes. You need to get out more."

"Tell me about it." Dakota glanced upward. "Your friend there would do for starters."

"Too bad he's taken."

Dakota wrinkled her face. "That won't last."

Molly peered closer. Dakota was serious. "What are you talking about? You've barely seen her."

Dakota confessed, "I saw enough. Your door there doesn't quite close all the way. Maybe it's a seasonal thing. The wood swells and then catches against my hand when I'm holding it open. You really ought to have Will take a look next time he's over here pining away for your mom."

"Shh!" Molly glared. "Don't let her hear you." A suspicious look came over Molly's face. "Hey, don't think you can distract me. You opened the door and spied on my guests."

Dakota recoiled. "Spying is such a strong word! It was more of an unsanctioned domestic surveillance operation."

Molly tried not to smile. It would only encourage her friend.

Dakota stared off into the distance. "I should name it."

"Name what?"

"My surveillance operation. If Zachary—or Zach, as I like to call him—is going to be staying here, I'll need a name for my spy operation."

"That is so inappropriate. You are not going to spy on him."

"Operation Carrera."

"Marble?"

"Car. Porsche Carrera. Black. Very classy."

"You looked at his car?" Molly was not enjoying the conversation nearly as much as Dakota seemed to be.

"I know. Cars aren't really my thing, except that one. It's so cute. So is he, by the way. If I have to be inappropriate with someone, he'll do."

"But you won't."

"Oh, I beg to differ." Dakota fluffed her hair. "I just need a little fresher-upper at the spa."

"That's not what I meant. I mean you won't have the chance to be inappropriate if I banish you from the inn for the duration of his stay."

Dakota heaved a sigh. "Well, okay. I see where we're going here. You saw him first. Finders keepers. Whatever."

Molly's eyes opened wide, but before she could protest, her friend laughed. "I knew he was yours from the start. You two had that magical eye contact thing going on."

"Oh, right. You mean that nanosecond when he glanced at me out of obligatory politeness."

"Magical eye contact has more of a ring to it, but okay."

Molly cast a chastising look at Dakota then noticed the piece of blank folded card stock before her. "How many Christmas cards have you finished?"

With halfhearted enthusiasm, Dakota rubber-stamped a piece of card stock and lifted it up and showed Molly. "This one's coming along. Pass the glitter glue?"

Molly silently worked on the card she was crafting. She had to agree that the new guest was handsome—strong facial planes, full lips, nice build.

"So what's the deal with the girlfriend?"

Molly looked up to find Dakota smiling and nodding. "You were thinking about him. You had that high school study hall dreamy-eyed daze."

Their eyes met, and Molly couldn't help grinning. "Well, okay. I won't deny that he's got a certain appeal." She came to her senses. "And a girlfriend. That's it. End of story."

"If you say so."

Molly set down her rubber stamp. "Look, how long have you known me?"

"Since fifth grade."

"Right. And what is the worst, most heartbreaking thing—" Molly stopped. The most heartbreaking thing was losing her father in her senior year. Nothing else came close to that. "What is the most heartbreaking romance-related thing that's ever happened to me?"

Dakota nodded. "The big breakup with The Jerk."

"Right. And why do we call him The Jerk?"

"Because he cheated on you. At a party you went to together."

There was no amusement left in Molly's eyes. "Correct. The world is full of jerks, but I don't have to be with them."

Dakota's lip was almost at full pout. "A girl can dream, can't she?"

"What for? Whatever you're thinking, it's not going to happen."

Molly had put more thought into that high school breakup than she would ever admit. It had left an impression on her and a firm resolve to avoid men like him in the future. "If someone cheats to get into a relationship, they'll cheat to get out of it, too. So I'm not going there."

Dakota lifted a sheepish face toward Molly. "But we can still look at him, right? From afar?"

Molly opened her mouth but couldn't find the words.

Dakota slumped. "I know. I need to get out more."

TWO

"Penelope, no!"

Zach put his hand over hers, which was gripping the doorknob. "A queen will be fine."

Penelope met his gaze with despair in her eyes. "I haven't slept in a queen-sized bed since I was a child."

"Sometimes life is so hard."

"Very funny." She yanked open the door and marched downstairs.

Zach closed his eyes and took in a breath before going after her. The poor desk clerk had no idea what was coming her way. He entertained the far-flung fantasy of Penelope walking straight through the front door and driving home. But that would mean her taking his car and leaving him stranded. In retrospect, driving separate cars would have solved so many problems. But he'd made some bad choices, and he had to live with them.

Being with Penelope had been an error in judgment—one of several he made after his first big sale. The car was another, but unlike Penelope, cars weren't unkind. It wasn't as though he hadn't planned. He'd realized early on that it wasn't going to work out with Penelope, so he made up his mind to break up with her after their Halloween party. But then her emergency surgery happened, and he couldn't dump her when she was down.

He shuddered as he recalled the evening.

PENELOPE HAD ARRIVED home with the costumes from the dry cleaners. They were rentals, so she insisted on having them cleaned first. She told him to put on something plain—jeans and a T-shirt would be fine. Then with a wave toward a large bag on the bed, she told him to pull on his costume over his outfit.

While he changed clothes, Zach reminded himself that he just needed to make it through one last evening, then tomorrow he'd break the news to her. It was over between them. He would take all the blame as he made his excuses. Work consumed him right now, and he wasn't in the right place in his life for a relationship.

Five minutes later, she emerged from the walk-in closet, looking gorgeous in a short and tight faux chain mail number complete with beguiling breastplate. While she twisted her hair into a knot, she said, "I just have to put on this short wig."

"You look gorgeous, but who are you dressed as?"

She pinned her wig into place and struck a pose. "Silly! I'm Sexy Joan of Arc."

Zach pulled a giant foam ear from the bag and held it up, puzzled.

"Hurry. Put it on. Our guests will arrive soon." She leaned close to the mirror and touched up her makeup.

Zach stared at the giant foam ear. "But what is it?"

"An ear. Duh."

"I can see that. But why?"

She had the same look she got with store clerks and waiters. "I'm Joan of Arc, and you're hearsay. Get it? Hear? An ear?" She rolled her eyes and heaved a huge sigh. "Joan of Arc was burned at the stake for hearsay."

Zach stared for a moment. "Heresy."

"Right. Hearsay." Penelope frowned disapprovingly.

In retrospect, Zach realized he should never have tried to explain the difference between hearsay and heresy to her. He should have just counted himself lucky she hadn't made him dress up as Joan of Arc's burning stake—a porterhouse, no doubt.

But they argued, and she started to whine that he'd given her a stomachache. Two hours later, burning with fever, she was in the midst of replenishing the hors d'oeuvres when she passed out. The resulting cloud of chip dust and pico de gallo had barely settled before paramedics arrived and whisked her away to the hospital. She was rushed into emergency surgery for a ruptured appendix. By the time she recovered, Thanksgiving was upon them. Not even Penelope deserved to be dumped during the holidays, so Zach had made a tough choice. Rather than ruin Penelope's holiday season, he would spare her feelings and ring in the new year before breaking up with her.

So HERE HE was on the vacation Penelope had surprised him with. The even bigger surprise was that he was paying for a vacation he didn't want to take. In the holiday spirit, he had gone along with it. Sparing her feelings was the right thing to do, but now he was miserable.

Zach followed Penelope downstairs to the front desk.

She rolled her eyes. "It figures. No one's here."

While Zach was relieved, Penelope glanced about

with mounting displeasure. "And no bell." She sighed and called out, "Hello?"

Zach tugged her by the elbow. "Come on. It's late. Let's not make a big thing out of this."

She turned and pointed her laser beam scowl at him. "Don't you think my comfort is a big thing?"

Zach shook his head slowly while formulating his answer.

Penelope's eyes widened. "I see." She looked past the desk toward the door to the kitchen then turned and headed to their room without him.

Zach stood and contemplated walking straight to his car and driving away, which was becoming a recurring dream, but the kitchen door opened.

"Oh!" Molly clutched her hand to her chest and smiled. "Sorry, you startled me."

"I'm sorry. It's late. I was just heading upstairs."

The light caught a speck of something on Molly's cheek. *Is that glitter?* She paused for a moment, looking confused. Why wouldn't she be? He was standing at the reception desk for no logical reason. Zach smiled. "Well, good night."

"Did you need something?"

"No, I was just heading back up to my room."

"But you must have come down here for something."

Zach said, "It's not important."

Molly's eyes clouded over. "It's important to me. Us. The inn."

He started to wave it off but found himself drawn to her warm, caring eyes. Her expression was one he wasn't used to seeing. "It's Penelope. But she wouldn't want to trouble you..." *Lying at Christmas? It's the bad list for you.* "But she was wondering if we might change at some point, when it's convenient, to a room with a king-sized bed." Molly's look of regret made him wish he hadn't said it, but he knew it sounded better coming from him than it would have from Penelope. She could be a little direct.

"Oh, I know it's an issue. But this old house has such small rooms that there really isn't space for a king. We've tried to make that clear on the website to avoid disappointment."

"I'm sure you have. Penelope actually made the reservation." *So she has only herself to blame.* As he glanced downward, he caught sight of the scissors in Molly's hand.

Molly followed his eyes and looked at the scissors, and her eyes crinkled as she smiled. "Oh. I don't always walk around carrying these. I was just putting them back in the drawer."

Something about her made him want to smile. "Good. I was going to double-check the sign out front to make sure it didn't say—"

"Bates Motel? Common mistake."

They laughed together, and a weight seemed to lift from his shoulders.

Molly said, "I assure you, this is the Christmas Tree Inn."

"Because of the trees in the yard?"

Molly's face lit up. "Yes, those and—you arrived after dark, so you must not have seen it. Next door, there's a Christmas tree farm. That came first, actually. This was just our house. But my mother turned it into an inn when I was young. I don't remember it as anything else."

"It's charming." *As are you.* Zach felt a sharp pang of guilt. "Well, good night."

"Good night, Mr. Moreton."

He corrected her. "Zach."

She smiled, and Zach left. But her green eyes and auburn hair pulled into a haphazard knot lingered in his thoughts as he walked up the stairs.

THREE

MOLLY SURVEYED the usual breakfast array of bagels and pastries. Satisfied with what she saw, she poured a fresh cup of coffee for herself and sank into a tall wingback chair facing the large fireplace that dominated the room. She loved this part of the day, when dawn was just breaking and guests were still snug in their beds. In twenty minutes, people would start trickling down from their rooms, but for now, the inn was all hers to enjoy.

Or not. Footsteps padded down the stairs and interrupted her moment of peace. Molly turned and started to stand.

"Don't get up. Please."

But she did. "Mr. Moreton. Good morning."

He lifted an admonishing eyebrow. "Zach, please."

Molly smiled. "Zach. Well, I'll leave you to your breakfast."

"I've interrupted you." His tone of sincere regret touched her.

"No, not at all. I like to sit by the fire for a few minutes in the mornings. It's only a coffee break. I was just finishing up here."

"Then please, don't let me stop you." That direct gaze of his was far too appealing for someone so sadly unavailable. He gestured toward the seat she had vacated. "Please."

She could have refused his invitation, but she returned to her seat as he'd suggested. Despite the half dozen tables scattered about, he chose to join her by the fire, in the chair next to hers. His eyes swept over the large fieldstone fireplace to the rest of the room. A wall of windows revealed a breathtaking view of Mount Mansfield, snow-covered and jutting up through the clouds as they clung to the spruces and balsam fir trees.

"I can see why you like this. Sitting inside by the fire with a beautiful view outside. It's everything I imagine when I think of getting away from the city. How lucky you must feel to live here."

Molly felt guilty. "I know. I mean, it's what I should feel, but it's what I grew up with, so to me it's just normal."

He leaned closer. "It's a very good normal. I wouldn't take this for granted."

She looked frankly at him. "I know. I do love it, but truth be told, I've dreamed of leaving here for as long as I can remember." *Molly, really. Sharing your hopes and dreams with a stranger? He's just making small talk.*

He regarded her as if she'd gone mad. "Why would you?"

Molly's mind went blank for a moment. "Why would I leave here? Well..." She'd almost started to share unnecessarily, and she was lost for something to tell him instead.

He looked away, embarrassed. "I'm sorry. I'm prying."

"No, you're not." He wasn't prying exactly. He was merely acting interested—something Molly didn't often encounter in her line of work. She was more used to being the invisible help—unless something was wrong. Then she was more visible than she wanted to be. Fortunately, their guests tended to be satisfied with their stays—except where king-sized beds were concerned.

Evading his inquiry, Molly said, "I take it Ms. Pomeroy is not a morning person."

That prompted an unexpected chuckle. "No, she is not. We'll be lucky to see her by noon."

"Oh, well, if you'd like some ideas for something to do in the meantime—"

"I'm fine right here, for now." He leaned back. "Would you mind sharing?"

I think I've done plenty of that.

He gestured toward the ottoman. It was large enough for two pairs of feet, yet something about sharing it seemed awfully personal. Molly brushed the thought aside. "Sure. I mean, no, I don't mind."

He leaned back and stared at the fire. Molly followed suit but managed to steal a good look at her guest. His hair wasn't as perfect as the day before, but it looked even better slightly tousled. He had the sort of masculine good looks that meant he couldn't help being just about everyone's type, but he was undeniably hers. His good looks were set off by the way he looked right at her with genuine interest. That was a drug she could get used to.

Moments passed in companionable silence. "I miss this." He took a sip of coffee. It almost sounded like he'd visited the inn before, but she would have remembered that. Before Molly could ask, he said, "I didn't know how much I missed it until I got here." He turned toward her and smiled gently. "I grew up in the country."

Surprised, Molly said, "That would have been my last guess."

"Really? Why?"

She had to come up with an answer that wouldn't include anything about snooty girlfriends. "I don't know. Nice suit? Sports car?"

He looked embarrassed. "The suit was just me coming straight from work, and the car was an error in judgment." He winced. "You see, I had this list. All through college, I was going to make money, buy a sports car, and have a high-rise apartment with windows that looked out over Manhattan."

And a stunning girlfriend—brains and manners optional. "Sounds nice."

He sighed. "Yeah, it is but—" He hesitated, apparently searching for words. "Sometimes I feel like I'm pretending to be someone I'm not."

Molly thought for a moment. "I think there's a name for that."

"Pretentious?"

Molly was charmed by his self-deprecation. "No. It's... imposter syndrome. Feeling like you don't deserve what you've earned."

"No, I don't think that applies. I've worked hard to get where I am, and I'm comfortable with it. But wearing success like a badge—or driving it, in my case —is just... well, it's just not who I am."

Molly studied him. "Who are you, then?" She started to lose herself in his eyes before her inner voice of reason reminded her to take a step back. She smiled lightly. "I mean, if you're not a sports car, what vehicle are you?" *Good save.*

"Hmm... an old pickup, I guess. No particular make or model as long as it's red. Not to be flashy but because it'll match the rust."

He might not want to be flashy, but his smile certainly was. Looking at it was like looking into the sun. *If you're losing control of your senses, which you seem to be. So snap out of it!*

"Good morning!" They both turned with a start. There she was, Ms. Penelope Pomeroy, looking as perfect as she did impatient. She looked through Molly then glared at Zach.

He smiled warmly. "You're up early."

Her eyes scanned the full length of him, sweater to jeans. "I thought we were skiing today."

"So we are. When you're finished with breakfast—"

"I'm finished."

With an awkward glance toward Molly, Zach stood. "Duty calls."

Molly smiled until her eyes drifted to Penelope. She swallowed.

"Duty? So now I'm a duty?" Penelope called after her boyfriend.

Her boyfriend. Remember that, Molly.

Zach was halfway to the stairs and didn't miss a step. "I'll just be a minute."

Ignoring Molly, Penelope calmly poured a cup of coffee and followed Zach up to their room.

As she rose and got on with her day, Molly couldn't help wondering how two people as different as Zach and Penelope could have wound up together. Opposites truly did attract.

Ten minutes later, Zach and Penelope descended the stairs, both in their ski clothes. They'd nearly reached the front door when Penelope said, "I'll just get a coffee to go."

While Zach waited, a woman with cropped gray hair walked in from the kitchen door behind the desk, carrying an armload of firewood. Zach sprang forward. "Here, let me help you."

"I'm fine. Thank you." As she spoke, her expression changed. "Actually, could you just take a few off the top? I might have been too ambitious."

"Sure." Zach took more than a few pieces off the top and carried them to a rack by the fireplace.

The woman brushed herself off and extended her hand. "You must be Mr. Moreton."

"Zach, please."

"Liz Foster."

Zach introduced Penelope, who deigned to offer a quick nod and smile as she stirred her coffee and put on a lid.

"You must have met Molly, my daughter, last night."

Now he could see the resemblance. Same height, same eyes. "Yes, we did."

"I trust everything's okay. If you need anything, let us know."

Penelope cleared her throat loudly.

Zach glanced at her then turned to Liz. "We're off to go skiing. It was nice meeting you, Liz."

"You, too, Zach."

As he walked to the car, Zach realized he hadn't been around people that warm and friendly—at least not strangers—in a long while. He missed it.

And whose fault is that?

Liz had just settled down at the front desk when Molly walked in from the kitchen. "Mom, we're running low on coffee creamers. Add that to the grocery list—oh." She stopped in her tracks as Zach opened the front door.

Molly checked her watch, thinking they couldn't

have been gone for more than an hour or two. "Back already?"

Zach turned and helped Penelope hobble inside wearing ill-fitting sweats and an orthopedic boot.

Liz gasped. "Oh no!"

Molly rushed over to hold the door open so Zach could give Penelope his full attention. Their eyes met, and she asked, "Ski accident?"

He gave his head a slight cautionary shake. "Not exactly."

Picking up on his cue, Molly didn't press further. She couldn't help noticing that Penelope seemed wobbly. "Has she—is she going to make it upstairs?"

"We'll manage. She just needs some support. The doctor gave her something for the pain."

It clearly had worked. From the looks of it, Penelope was feeling no pain. Zach was another story. He had a pain in his arms, and her name was Penelope. Molly chastised herself for the snarky thought. Ms. Pomeroy was a guest and, as such, deserved her respect and hospitality.

Zach started to carry Penelope up the stairs, but when he turned to avoid hitting her foot in the narrow space, he came dangerously close to bumping her head on the opposite wall. He set her back on her feet, but Penelope's knees buckled. Zach repositioned his arm about her waist.

"Here, let me help you." Molly pulled Penelope's arm over her shoulder. He did the same, and the two of them managed to get her up the stairs and into bed.

As Zach pulled a blanket over his girlfriend, Molly noticed the strained look in his eyes. Poor guy. He'd had quite an afternoon. Moved by pity, Molly said, "Can I get you something? A beer? A general anesthetic?"

He turned and laughed, then he looked down at Penelope. An abrupt snort startled them both.

Silence settled, which Molly took as her cue to leave. "I'll bring something up. Have you eaten?"

Still looking at Penelope, he shook his head.

"We'll take care of that." Molly left.

A FEW MINUTES LATER, Zach closed the door gently and headed downstairs. As he rounded the foot of the staircase, he practically ran straight into Molly, nearly upending the tray she was carrying. He reached out to steady the tray, inadvertently putting his hand over hers. With the tray well stabilized, he quickly slid his hand away. *Soft skin*, he noted.

"I decided to eat here. She's down for the count, and I didn't want to disturb her, so I left her with her phone in her hand. If she wakes up, she won't hesitate to use it." He grinned.

Liz, still at work at the front desk, glanced over her glasses and smiled at Zach then returned to her paperwork. While Molly set the tray's contents on a table for him, he asked, "Care to join me?"

She smiled. "Thanks. I've eaten."

"Coffee break?"

When she hesitated, Zach looked up and said, "To be honest, I could use some company."

Her eyebrows drew together, then a smile teased at her lips. "Be right back."

She returned with a coffee and sat down across from him. Through the frost on the window beside them, the snow glistened, casting a soft glow on her skin. *This isn't something I should be noticing.* He dismissed the thought.

"I take it Ms. Pomeroy took a tumble on the slopes."

He hesitated. "No, we didn't quite make it to the slopes."

Molly looked surprised and confused. He knew he wasn't helping, but he wasn't quite sure how to describe what had happened. He took a breath and forged onward. "She had her little fold-up mirror in her hand. She likes to check her makeup whenever she enters a new space. Something to do with the lighting?

Anyway, in the middle of the ski resort's lobby, there's a fountain with a skylight above."

Molly nodded. "I know the place."

"She later told me she was trying to get into the best light." He looked up at Molly's curious, very-green eyes. "Which was apparently over the water. And..." He winced. "She leaned a little too far and did a face plant in the fountain. Which reminds me, I left her wet clothes in the car. I'll need to hang them up."

"Bring them to me. I'll take care of them."

"That's above and beyond."

Molly leveled a no-nonsense look at him. "It's no big deal. We've got a washer and drier."

"Oh no. She's very particular about laundry."

Molly nodded. "We've got a rack. I'll just hang them up to dry."

"Thank you." He wondered how this woman, whom he barely knew, managed to put him at ease. If Penelope were sitting across from him, his mind would be racing as he tried to anticipate what might upset her next. And that was why he was breaking up with her—after the holidays. A pleasant Christmas with no drama, that was all that he wanted. But sitting here having feelings for somebody else was bad form. He was going to have to remind himself of this when he was with Molly Foster.

"Falling into a fountain in winter... That can't have

been pleasant." Molly's eyes crinkled, and she looked confused. "But how did she hurt her ankle?"

Zach sought a tactful way to explain what had happened. "When she got out of the water, she slipped."

He left out the part about how she had risen from the water like a fuming sea creature and begun shouting orders at him and the ski lodge employees who had already scrambled to her aid. With their help, she got back on her feet, her pink ski outfit dripping and her hair hanging in highlighted clumps.

Penelope was no stranger to anger, but a new level of rage burned in her eyes as she took a sudden step toward the door to storm out, and she slipped, falling backward. How she managed to get her leg trapped underneath her was a testimony to the force of the fall and her hot yoga–induced flexibility. Minutes later, an ambulance had arrived and whisked her away to the nearby hospital.

"And she fell."

Seeing Molly's sympathetic reaction, Zach nodded. "They checked out her back and did a brain scan in case she injured her head when she fell. Fortunately, she's only mildly concussed, and her ankle is sprained."

"Oh. Well, that's not so bad."

"No, not at all. If you'd seen the whole thing, you'd have expected far worse."

"Still, I'm sorry it happened."

"I wanted to take her home, but the doctor advised her to take it easy for a couple of days until the concussion symptoms subsided."

Zach noticed Molly's cup was empty. He glanced at the one-cup coffee machine on the breakfast buffet. "Can I get you a refill?"

Molly smiled. "I'd better get back to work before the boss notices me slacking off."

"She's aware," said a voice from across the room. Still at work at the front desk, Liz shot a look at Molly with twinkling eyes.

Molly grinned. "See? No rest for the weary. Or is it *wicked*?"

"You don't look either. Just nice."

Feeling a blush coming on, Molly winced.

He added, "But in a smart, capable, and interesting way."

With a glint in her eyes, she said, "You're very good."

"Why would I lie?" *Why would I have to?* He'd managed to make that sound far too serious. Or perhaps it was the way emotions he hadn't expected were now so close to the surface.

Neither moved.

He wasn't sure how she did it. He barely knew her, but she put him at ease. While six months with Penelope had given him more than enough practice at saying the right things, talking to Molly was effortless. He just said what he was thinking—except for the part about wishing he'd been able to break up with Penelope when the thought had first occurred to him. He was thinking about that quite a bit.

"Well! That's done!" Liz said cheerily, if a little too loudly.

Molly flinched then covered with a broad smile. "Time for me to get back to work!" She stood, grabbed his plate and cutlery, and whisked them away to the kitchen. Liz followed.

"Don't say it." Molly hastened to load the dishwasher.

"I didn't say anything." Liz cast a look at her daughter and continued to her room.

But her mom had that look, like she could read Molly's mind and know what she was thinking, although it didn't take much mind reading when Molly was in the same room, practically giggling and blushing like someone in a Jane Austen novel. Molly gripped the edge of the counter. *It's nothing. He'll be gone in a couple of days.* She picked up a rag and wiped down the counter, which was already clean. *Everything's fine.*

The best thing, Molly decided, was to avoid Zach. This was all just a sign that she'd spent too much time in this small rural community. If one attractive city boy in a suit could turn her head so easily, she needed more of a life. But it wasn't as if tourists didn't swarm the region at this time of year. They'd had more than their share of guests from cities all over the Northeast. Why should Zachary Moreton be so different?

More than one guest had tried to charm her. A few had attempted to carry it further. She'd made that mistake only once. She had no interest in a romance that ended at checkout time, so she would not let it happen again. Once she'd learned how duplicitous some men could be, it was easy to recognize the telltale signs and avoid them.

But Zach was different. For one thing, he was here with his girlfriend. That was different enough. And it was reason enough to go running in the other direction. She had no business being so attracted to him. Molly smiled to herself. It wasn't his fault. He hadn't asked for that face, although that body was no accident. That took some work at the gym. But there was nothing wrong with being healthy. Or handsome.

FOUR

MOLLY MANAGED to avoid Zach for the rest of the day. The next morning, she finished setting up breakfast and sat by the fire, feeling calm and in control. Her moment of peace was interrupted when Will, the Christmas tree farm manager and resident plowman, pulled into the driveway to clear the night's snowfall. She stood at the window and watched as the plow cut a path through the new-fallen snow. She loved the snow in December. January was another story. But for now, there was nothing better than looking out at the fresh snow while a fire blazed inside.

After Will had run a landscaping business for years, his wife became ill, so he sold the business and retired early to spend time with her. Being with her became caring for her in the end. For a few years, he confined himself to his mountain cabin, coming out only for groceries and other necessities. But a good friend, Molly's father, drew him out under the guise of needing help on the Christmas tree farm. Her father always needed help, but Will needed it more.

When Molly's father unexpectedly died, Will took over the running of the farm. In the years that followed, Molly began to suspect that Will's feelings for her mother were growing beyond friendship. Liz balked if Molly even hinted at it, but Will was always there, looking after them in his quiet way.

Molly missed the old days when her father was alive. Her parents were such a great team. Molly's father was the tree expert, while Liz's strength was providing a comfortable home away from home for guests while keeping a close eye on the business side of their joint enterprise. When things broke down, her dad always knew how to fix them. Will picked up most of the slack in that department, and Molly had acquired some skills here and there. She could tile, paint, and replace the odd faucet, but she wouldn't go near an electrical repair. That was where Will stepped in. Maybe he was just being a friend, but Molly wondered.

She turned from the window. There she was again, speculating over things that were none of her business. One thing she did know was that Will would come inside for his usual morning coffee as soon as the plowing was finished. And Liz would greet him, just as she did every morning. As far as Molly could tell, no words had been spoken to redefine what they were to each other. She'd seen no longing looks exchanged. And yet there was something. She couldn't quite pinpoint it, but she sensed it. It hovered in the air like Christmas magic—intriguing, even fascinating, but best left undisturbed. That was just how it was and would remain.

The floor creaked at the top of the stairs, prompting Molly to make a mad dash for the kitchen. If she didn't see him, she wouldn't feel attracted to him, and soon he would leave. Problem solved. But her mother walked through the door before she could reach it.

"Oh, I forgot. Would you bring me the cinnamon while you're in there? I feel like having some in my coffee. Look at me being wild and adventurous!" Liz laughed and sat down at the desk.

Molly pulled the cinnamon out of the cupboard. *Cinnamon? What's that about?* Her mother was too old to start changing things up. But Molly had more important things to worry about, because now she had to go back into the reception room and risk seeing Zach. *Molly, look at yourself. You're an adult.* She exhaled and ventured forth into the unknown, armed with a small bottle of ground cinnamon. And there he was.

"Good morning." Zach stood up from the tall front desk he'd been leaning casually against while he chatted with her mother. Clearly, they were having a more relaxed morning than she.

"Oh, hi." *Good job, Molly. Very blasé. Now smile pleasantly. Good. Are your eyes shining? Look away. Look. Away.* She handed the cinnamon to her mother. *Now to escape with a quick "Have a nice day."* But that would have been too easy.

Liz sprinkled cinnamon into her coffee. "Zach was just telling me Penelope's feeling better."

Subtle, Mom. Got it. He's taken. "Oh, that's great. Glad to hear it." *That means you'll be leaving, and after a cold shower, I'll be as good as new.*

"But her head's still feeling tingly, so she's spending the day in bed, watching TV."

"Would she like something to read? Those books on the shelves by the fireplace are for guests. Help yourself."

Zach's eyes sparkled as though he might burst into laughter. "Penelope's not much of a reader."

"Oh." *There's a shocker.*

"She'll be fine binge-watching reality shows."

"That sounds good." She nodded as if she believed it.

"Yeah." Zach looked miserable, but of course he had to be miserable. His girlfriend had gotten hurt on the first day of their visit. Their romantic escape had been ruined. Poor them.

Zach's phone dinged. He studied it, looking displeased. Abruptly, he looked up with a bright expression that didn't reach his eyes. "There she is now." His lips spread halfway to a smile. "See you later."

"Bye." Molly and her mother watched with blank looks on their faces.

As Zach mounted the stairs, Will came in from the kitchen. "Morning!" He was in his socks, having slipped off his boots in the mudroom per his usual morning routine. He strode straight to the coffee then went to the fireplace, where he liked to sit and prop his feet up on the ottoman. "On a cold, snowy day like today, it's tempting to just stay here and never leave."

Molly studied her mom for a reaction but saw none.

Liz looked up from the computer. "You're welcome to come back when you're done plowing, but you'll probably be hungry, and we only serve breakfast."

His eyes twinkled. "Then I'll have to bring lunch."

"Suit yourself." Liz feigned indifference, but Molly knew her mother too well. The woman was perfectly capable of speaking up for herself. She could have come up with any number of excuses on the spot, like, "That sounds lovely, but my explosive diarrhea is acting up" or "Sorry, but I've got to wax my moustache." But she hadn't. She just went ahead and made plans for lunch, which made it a great day to go elsewhere for lunch. Molly would go into the village. She could work in some exercise as she walked from store to store and checked off items on her holiday gift list. The snow had let up, so the roads would be clear.

Two hours later, she had finished her morning chores, changed clothes, and started driving to the village. Pleased by the chance for some time to herself, she passed by her usual lunch spot, a favorite of the locals. She would inevitably run into someone there, so she settled on the Bake & Brew Café in the middle of the village. It was a small homespun place tucked inside a large barn-colored building along with an independent book store and a gift shop, all of which gave it a Vermont country store vibe. As she went in from the cold, the sudden warmth combined with the smell of freshly baked goods reminded her why the place was her favorite village stop on a wintry day.

With fortuitous timing, Molly saw a couple get up from a table close to the wood stove, so she slipped in and ordered hot soup and a slice of homemade bread while the table was being cleared. Once alone, Molly pulled out her phone and lost herself in a novel. In the midst of her book-reading daze, footsteps approached, so she moved her phone to make room for her lunch plate. But instead of her lunch, she looked up to find Zach.

He looked warm and friendly, as always. "It is you. I wasn't sure. You looked so intense."

"That's my usual look." Molly smiled. "I was reading a book."

"Would you mind if I joined you? I'm not staying. I just put in a take-out order, so you'd be rid of me soon."

"Sure." Molly gestured toward the chair his hand rested upon.

Zach sat down and leaned back with an ease she found not only disarming but also in marked contrast to her own unease. She'd seen that sort of confidence. It wasn't the arrogant or presumptuous kind. He just knew who he was and was comfortable with it. That might be because he always seemed more concerned about the comfort of others than his own. Given that, the one thing she didn't get about him was Penelope. Molly did not understand that pairing.

Something bumped against her ankle.

"Oh! Sorry. That was my clumsy foot." He made a face that, while meant to be funny, still managed to be attractive. That prompted Molly to wonder whether she'd developed a stupid crush filter that made everything he did look too appealing. She wished he'd do something gross—like clean his earwax with his finger—to put her theory to the test.

Molly laughed as though his little kick in the ankle were nothing, which didn't explain why she pulled her feet back so quickly that, if ankles got whiplash, hers would have been wearing braces. It wasn't as though a mere touch would spark an explosion. It was only her heart that was at risk. And at the moment, her heart was in danger of melting. One more touch and she would slide off her chair and disappear like the Wicked Witch of the West.

Zach asked about her book, so they chatted about it. Then he studied her for a moment. "So, have you always wanted to be an innkeeper?"

"No." That came out too quickly.

He lifted an eyebrow. "Then what did, or do, you want to be when you grow up?" He grinned.

Molly's smile bloomed and faded. "I was all set to go to college. But in the spring of my senior year, my father died."

"I'm sorry." It was one of those things people said. What else was there to say? But their eyes met, and he seemed to lack the usual awkward desire to change the subject. "How?"

"Heart attack. Mom was devastated, of course. I was lost. But we coped, because that's what you do. You keep moving, and time passes." She was about to move on to something else when the unexpected grip of emotion seized her. She averted her eyes. "Sorry. That hardly happens anymore—at least not in public— with strangers." She lifted her palm and smiled. "I'm okay." But her eyes still felt moist.

"Yes, you are."

His steady gaze was too much to bear. Anyone else would have spared her by looking away.

He said simply, "I lost my father when I was in college."

Their eyes met, and they shared a moment of understanding. Neither needed to voice it.

Their food arrived at the same time, Zach's in a sack on the table. "Perfect timing. You're spared my sad story."

Molly smiled. "But the ending is happy, right?"

He looked as though he wanted to say something to her, but he grinned and said, "Right," then slid out of the booth and wished her a good afternoon.

MOLLY STOMPED the snow from her boots and walked into the kitchen. There they were, her mother and Will, at the kitchen table and looking very relaxed over coffee. It still took her by surprise when she happened upon them together. For an instant, she would think it was her father, even though it couldn't possibly be. But the heart played tricks on the mind. As the possibility of her mother and Will grew more real, Molly began to understand how alone her mother must feel. Molly shifted her focus from her father, for whom nothing could change, to her mother, who needed a change. She deserved to be happy, so it was up to Molly to support whatever would make her mom happy. Maybe it wasn't that different from how her mother would feel if Molly found someone to love. Still, Molly thought, that sort of unselfishness was harder for children than for parents. Children had spent their lives being the focus of their parents. The world revolved around them. Adult children had to grow into their unselfish feelings. Molly would get there in time.

She went upstairs, rummaged through the attic, and brought down some boxes. On her third and last trip, she stepped down off the bottom step and set down the last box of Christmas decorations. As she brushed her hair back from her forehead, Penelope's voice rang out through the nearby closed door. "So you sat down with her and had a nice chat while I waited here starving?"

Zach answered in a low, indecipherable murmur, then something struck the door. The next moment, it opened. Molly froze. Zach stood in the doorway, partially blocking Penelope's feet and the lower half of the bed, the rest of the bed mercifully hidden from view. He quickly stepped outside and closed the door behind him. "I'm sorry."

"I was just getting the Christmas decorations down from the attic." *I'll be disappearing now.* She picked up a box and headed toward the stairs, leaving two other boxes behind.

"Let me help you."

"No, really. I can get it."

But he had already picked up a box with garland springing out between overlapped folds of cardboard on top. He followed her downstairs and sprinted back up for the last one. As he set down the final box, Molly practically buried her face in the first one and preoccupied herself with the task of unpacking and sorting.

"Thanks!" She barely glanced in his direction.

Zach didn't leave. When she couldn't stand it anymore, Molly looked up at him.

"That was..." He paused as if searching for words.

She shook her head dismissively. There was no use in pretending it hadn't happened when they both knew it had.

"Embarrassing."

Molly looked at him directly, but it pained her to do so. "It's okay."

"No. It isn't."

He'd lost his earlier confidence, but even in this miserably awkward moment, he seemed more concerned about Molly.

Liz walked in. "Ready to decorate?"

Perhaps it was the same thing that made a person want to laugh during church, but the two of them suddenly burst into laughter, leaving Liz looking confused.

Zach asked, "May I help?"

At the same time Molly said, "No," Liz said, "Sure!"

Liz looked at each of the boxes. "Why don't you two fish out the lights from that box?" So they went to the box at the bottom of the stairs and began to unpack.

Molly looked up from her tangle of lights. "Are you sure this is what you need to be doing right now?"

Never had a man looked so sure. "Yes. It's exactly what I need to be doing."

The three of them wrapped garland on the banister, strung lights in the windows, and hung garland on the mantel.

Zach pulled a thick stack of stockings from one of the boxes. "There must be two dozen here."

Liz said, "We save those for last."

Molly smiled. "Mom collects Christmas strays."

"Cats?"

"No, people."

"Not on purpose," Liz explained. "It's just something that's evolved. Over the years, we've gotten to know some of our regulars. Things happen, and I never like the idea of people being alone over the holidays, so we began to invite them for Christmas. Some of them found friends to spend the day with, and others came once or twice. And then, one year, life happened to me." Liz teared up.

Molly finished the story. "And they all came for Christmas. They came loaded with gifts, groceries, and recipes. And they cooked and made Christmas happen. And it kind of became a tradition." She glanced at the pile of stockings in Zach's hands. "We're never really sure how many there'll be, so we wait and hang the stockings on Christmas Eve."

"That sounds…" Zach's phone buzzed.

"Different?" asked Molly.

Zach put the stockings in their box, then he pulled his phone from his pocket. "No, perfect." He glanced at his phone. "So much for perfect." He flashed a smile at Liz. "Thank you."

Liz laughed. "For letting you help?"

Zach nodded. "Yes." He tossed a grin Molly's way and climbed the stairs.

FIVE

MOLLY HURRIED to lay out the continental breakfast before her mother arrived. She had swapped desk duty with her under the guise of needing a breakfast meeting over Dakota's latest boyfriend emergency. The truth was that Molly needed some time away from the inn to gather her Zach-addled wits. Times like this reminded her of how sheltered her life had been these past few years since her father had died. She'd never lived on her own and made her own decisions. Her dating life was limited. She knew better, yet here she was letting her heart soar when she should have been cautious. She'd allowed herself to imagine some romantic interest from a guest who was merely being nice. At least she had the good sense to know that she needed some time—a few hours away—to clear her head.

Molly parked and walked half a block down the main street. All the stores and streetlights were in full Christmas splendor, which lifted her spirits. When she walked into the bakery, Dakota was already seated. Molly sat down and took in a deep breath. "They're baking Christmas magic back there."

"Not magic enough to be calorie-free."

Molly laughed. "No, that would be some powerful magic."

Dakota picked up her phone and set an alarm. "We've got twenty-eight minutes before I have to leave for work, and I want to hear everything, so go." She pointed at Molly.

"No pressure."

"Tell me what happened. Did he drown her in a vat of eggnog? No, that would be too good for her. Maybe she looked so far down her nose she fell over backward."

Molly's eyebrows drew together. "When did you meet Penelope?"

"That two-second glimpse with the door open a crack was enough. She's not hard to figure out. And you've shared a few stories."

"Yeah, well, she's a unique individual."

Dakota looked at her watch. "I don't care about her. Tell me about him."

"I've lost my mind."

Dakota fixed her eyes on Molly. "Did I ask about you? No. I asked about him. So...he's hot. But we know that already. Tell me more."

"He's with someone."

Dakota rolled her eyes. "Oh yeah. Her."

Molly stared at her coffee. "I know. She may not be the nicest human being."

"Aren't you the astute judge of character?" Dakota tore off a piece of doughnut and ate it.

"But she's his human being, and he's hers. So I can't have him. One of life's disappointments."

Dakota sighed. "Reminds me of so many Christmases."

Molly wrinkled her face. "What?"

"Presents. Turns out, Santa doesn't always deliver what you ask for. Which is a crying shame, 'cause that Zach would look great in a big Christmas bow." She muttered, "Word to the wise: watch where you place those. That little adhesive card smarts. Not that I'd know firsthand."

"This isn't really helping."

Dakota frowned sympathetically. "I know. But the thing is, I'm not sure there is any help for it."

"I guess I knew that already. I just wanted to talk." Molly lifted her hopeless eyes.

Dakota glanced at her watch. "Talk away. You've got seven minutes. Spill your guts."

Molly laughed.

Dakota took the last sip of coffee and set down her mug. "Look, the thing is, he might very well find you attractive, but what kind of guy dumps his girlfriend— who's here with him, during the holidays, no less—for a fun fling with you?" Dakota's eyebrows furrowed. "The kind of guy I've probably dated."

Molly shook her head.

"View him like you'd view a handsome actor in a movie. It's never really the actor, is it? It's the character you fall in love with. The one you've imagined. Real actors are... well, they're probably still hot, but they're never as interesting as the characters they play. Not even close."

"Okay?" Molly saw where she was going. She just didn't want to go there.

"You barely know Zach. You know a few facts, and you've filled in the blanks. You've imagined him like you want him to be, but it's probably not who he actually is. Just like those guys in the movies. In real life, at this moment, name any actor. Is he longing for someone with smoldering eyes? No. He's probably having a facial while whining about traffic and dialing his agent to bitch about how they stocked his trailer with the wrong color candy."

"Maybe... I guess."

Dakota's alarm went off. "Oops. Gotta go!"

"Oh, don't be late!"

"I won't. I built in a one-minute cushion in case you were distraught."

She leaned closer and peered in Molly's eyes. "Call or text anytime."

"I will."

MOLLY WALKED in from breakfast with Dakota to find Liz finishing up a phone call. "Two of Will's workers called in. There's a flu bug going around the high school, and they've caught it. He'd heard something was going around, so it wasn't a total surprise, but they'd all hoped the tree farm would escape it."

Molly said, "Let me change. I'll head over."

"I was hoping you'd say that."

"Sorry, but I couldn't help but overhear." Zach turned and peeked around the chair he'd been slumped down in near the fire.

Molly was already gone when Liz said, "'Tis the season."

"You said two workers called in."

"Yes. Poor things. And poor Will."

"Molly can't cover two people."

"She'll have to."

Zach got up and walked over to Liz. "I'll help."

"That's so nice of you, but I won't hear of it."

"You won't have to. I'll be well out of earshot." He grinned.

"You're a guest. This is your vacation."

"Yeah, but those plans kind of went south on day one." He lifted his eyes toward his upstairs room. "Frankly, I could use a distraction."

Molly returned in her cold-weather gear. "Hi, Zach. Mom, see you later."

"Wait, I'm coming with you." Zach bounded up the stairs.

Molly's eyes narrowed. "What's he talking about?"

Liz shook her head. "He insists on helping out next door."

"No."

"I tried to tell him."

He hurried down the stairs and pulled on his knit cap. "Ready?"

"Yes, but you're not."

Zach looked down at his jacket and the gloves in his hand. "I think I am."

Molly was stern—or at least she thought she was. "You are not going to work at the Christmas tree farm."

"Why not?"

"Because you don't know how to."

Zach was not getting the message. "Don't know how to do what?"

"Be outdoorsy."

"Oh? Watch me." He left without her.

"Mom, do something."

With a helpless expression, Liz said, "I could make some homemade soup and a fresh loaf of bread. That would taste good after working outside." Liz went into the kitchen.

Molly put her palm to her forehead. "What is happening here?"

ZACH LOADED the top of a car with a tree then went inside to warm up. Molly rang up a customer on the register and wished her a Merry Christmas. When she went out the door, Molly said, "I thought Will said it wouldn't be busy."

"The school district called a snow day, so all the kids were out of school. When the bad weather failed to materialize, the whole village seemed to decide this would be the perfect day to come get a tree. At least, that's what one customer told me."

As more shoppers approached, Zach winked and said, "I'd better get back to work before the boss sees me chatting you up."

He was on his way outside when a customer

approached him. "Would you please help me cut down a tree?"

"Sure, which one?" Zach grabbed a bow saw and started following the man.

"How's everything going?" Will joined Molly, who was far too busy watching Zach to have noticed his approach.

"Will!"

"Yes!" he echoed.

"Would you take the register?"

"Sure, but why?"

Molly was already halfway to Zach, leaving Will with a line at the register. She finally caught up with Zach at the tree. "I can take it from here."

Zach turned to her. "Molly?"

She smiled at a young girl waiting with her mother. "Excuse me." She pulled Zach aside. "I got this. You can go back to your station."

"My station? I didn't know I had one."

Molly leaned closer to avoid making a scene, but it was too late for that.

Zach folded his arms, his eyes lit with amusement. "You don't think I can do it."

"I didn't say that... exactly."

He handed over the saw. "By all means. I'll just watch and learn from a master."

What's that supposed to mean? She wished he

would stop staring. But she would not let him see she was rattled. "Okay."

She bent down and started to saw but was met with some resistance. "This tree's kind of sappy."

He turned to the customer. "Like some of my friends." They both chuckled.

Molly's saw got stuck. "Zach, would you grab the tree, please, and pull away from me?"

"Sure." He asked the customer's daughter to help while he winked at the mother. He told the child to pull his arm while he pulled on the tree. By the time Molly finished the job, she rose, red-faced and clearly frustrated, but put on her best holiday smile for the mother and child, both of whom barely noticed her since they were so charmed by Zach.

He carried the tree to the register to ring it up and prepare it for the trip home. On the way, he told Molly, "I forgot how long it takes to cut down a tree."

Molly scowled.

Once the tree was shaken, baled, and tied onto the top of the car, Zach waved goodbye. The little girl said, "That was fun." The mom smiled at Zach and drove off.

When they got back to the register, Will asked, "Would one of you help this man with a tree?"

Feeling the need to explain, the customer said, "I

came straight from work, and I don't want to mess up my suit."

"No problem," Zach said. Then he turned to Molly. "Since I'm still in training, would you please come along and assess my technique?"

Molly hesitated and studied his face but couldn't get a good read. He looked earnest. They were both waiting for her, so she said, "Okay."

When they arrived at the tree, Zach bent down and made a few strokes that looked like he was cutting through butter. Less than a half minute later, he was done.

Molly smiled at the customer then turned to Zach. "You look like you can manage from here." She cast an icy look toward Zach and did her best to walk briskly away, but she tripped on a tree stump.

Zach rushed over and caught her. Before he could ask, she snapped, "I'm okay," and walked away, scanning the ground for stray stumps.

When the last customer walked out the door, Will high-fived Molly and Zach. "We did it! You two can go. I just have to close out the register."

So they left and walked halfway to the inn. Zach broke the strained silence. "Molly—"

"So you can cut trees. Good for you."

"I told you I grew up on a farm."

"You told me you grew up in the country. There's a difference."

"You're right."

Molly walked faster, but Zach kept pace with her. "So I assumed..."

"And you were wrong."

"Yeah, and did you ever show me."

She marched away, but he caught up to her. "I was just having some fun."

"Oh, really? I wasn't. And by the way, that tree just happened to have a lot of sap, so it slowed me down."

"Sap happens. But you overcame it."

Molly didn't know how to take that. She was sure there had to be a hidden insult in there somewhere, but she couldn't find it. Still unsure whether to trust him, she said, "Thank you" and kept narrow eyes on him.

"You're welcome. And I'm sorry. I grew up on a farm. I milked cows, drove a tractor. The usual stuff. If there's anything else you want to know about me, just ask."

He was awfully agreeable. She couldn't think of one thing to ask. Instead, all she could think of was how condescending she had been to him and how he might not have deserved it. "It's just that you're so darned frustrating."

"Is that a question?"

"Oh, sorry." She should never have looked up at

him. If she had only walked away, she would have avoided seeing the soft look in his eyes. It disarmed her. They stood face-to-face in the moonlight. A light turned on from a second-floor window and cast a soft glow on the snow about them. Molly and Zach looked up, and Penelope was in the window.

They both turned from each other as though they'd been caught doing something they shouldn't have been. Picking up the pace, the two walked to the inn and went their separate ways.

SIX

Molly was on desk duty when Penelope, with Zach's assistance, hobbled down the stairs. "Ugh, I couldn't stand another minute in that small, dreary room."

Molly frowned. Theirs was the best room the inn had to offer. She'd always found it quite charming with its window seats, built into the two dormer windows, and its exposed beams, which were original to the historic building. It was furnished with a mahogany sleigh bed covered in crisp white bedding three deep in Egyptian cotton pillows propped against the headboard. Years ago, her father had even added an en suite bath with a Carrara marble vanity top and tiles. But if Penelope thought that was dreary, so be it.

Zach cast a look of silent apology Molly's way, and she forced a smile in return.

To her good fortune, Liz missed Penelope's

comment and walked in from the kitchen with a fresh supply of coffee-brewing cups for the buffet. "Well, look who's out and about!"

Penelope heaved a deep sigh. "Thank God!"

Liz arranged the coffee cups and walked over to the desk. "Molly, I'm going to make a quick run into the village for some Christmas gift shopping."

"Oh! May I come along?" Penelope seldom looked like she needed anyone, but at the moment, she looked like an eager show puppy.

A muzzle would be inhumane. Molly wasn't proud of the thought, but at least she hadn't said it out loud.

Liz smiled, but Molly recognized the blank smile that she used when she was thinking of a gracious way to squirm out of something unpleasant. "Doesn't that sound a little ambitious for that ankle of yours?"

Oh, that was excellent, Mom!

"That's what this boot is for. It'll give me support, while the walking will strengthen my ankle." Apparently, Penelope did know how to smile warmly. Molly had just never seen it before.

Only a slight hint of panic appeared in her mother's eyes. Molly smiled. But Penelope looked awfully confident. Molly came to Liz's aid, thinking that if they double-teamed her, they might stand a chance. "I'm sure you'd have more fun shopping with Zach." This was Zach's cue to chime in, but he didn't.

Penelope smiled at Zach. "Oh, we've tried that." She leaned closer to Liz and said quietly, "It's like shopping with a ten-year-old boy."

Zach added, "Or an adult who hates shopping."

Penelope burst into giggles. "Oh, Zach, you're so funny! Would you go get my jacket and purse?"

"Sure." His pleasant tone rang false to Molly, who suspected he would be relieved to be rid of her, if only for a few hours. Or maybe that was just Molly projecting her own feelings on the situation.

Despite her sympathy for her mother, Molly looked forward to a few hours of peace. But the dream faded when she found herself face-to-face with the law of unintended consequences. She and Zach would be alone in the inn.

Her face brightened. "Well, now you've got time for a walk. Or the slopes, since you never made it the last time. What a glorious day for it."

He didn't look nearly as eager as she. "I might go for a walk. Want to join me? I hear it's a glorious day."

Molly sighed. "I can't. I've got to hold down the fort."

His eyes twinkled as he gave her a look of mock pity. "Too bad. I'll just go get my jacket."

On his way down, he said, "See you later" and went on his way.

Molly relaxed. She was not managing her feelings

well. Each moment with him sent her deeper and deeper into... no. As long as she did not put words to it, it didn't exist. *Falling? Who's falling? Girl, you're hanging on by a thread.*

Thirty minutes later, Molly had paid some bills, said goodbye to the maid who had finished for the day, and begun to lose herself in a novel. There was even a moment or two when she didn't think of Zach. That was progress.

Then the door opened. "Miss me?"

Molly laughed lamely. "I managed."

"What are you reading?"

She casually lifted her book in one hand. "Oh, this? It's a book."

As if that were news, he nodded. "I see. You must be due for a coffee break. Black, right?"

Without waiting for her answer, he went straight to the coffee. Her mind raced as she sought an excuse to decline. But she couldn't claim she had work to do. She was sitting here reading a novel, for fudge cake. She couldn't say she had somewhere to go. He already knew she was stuck here on duty. "Yeah." That feeble sound she heard was her voice. *Good job nipping this in the bud. You sure set him straight. Why, that was just one step away from a WWE smackdown.*

They sat in the same seats where they'd sat by the fire before, as if they were assigned.

Zach sipped his coffee. "This is so good after being outside."

He looked content. She'd seen contentment before, but it looked even better with a square jaw and stubble. And that thick light-brown hair didn't hurt. Her heart did, but that was her fault. There was no denying that she had a crush. But it was only a side effect of living a secluded life in the woods.

"So." Zach turned sideways, faced her, and rested his elbow on the back of the chair. "You never did tell me what you wanted to be when you grow up."

"Oh. Didn't I? Well…" He didn't waste any time. Jumped right in, straight to the feelings. "Nothing special. I just wanted to go to college."

He waited and listened—a dangerous skill. It led Molly to continue.

"But I went to college online, so it all worked out."

"That's not quite the same."

"I missed a few keg parties, and I'm the only one in my generation who's never played beer pong, but I've survived." She smiled, but he didn't.

"What would you have done if things had been different?"

Molly was beginning to feel as though he might be manipulating her to throw her off balance and make her vulnerable. Or he was just being nice, and she was in the throes of a crush-induced paranoid delusion. It wasn't his fault that she couldn't resist finding him attractive. But frankly, it was exhausting. And he was still waiting for an answer.

"I like what I'm doing, a lot. I do. But I guess I'd like to be independent for once, just to know what it's like and to know that I can do it. Sometimes, I feel like I'm living my parents' dream instead of my own."

She wondered why he wasn't talking. It was his turn. But his eyes were on hers, and she couldn't look away.

Someone needed to talk, so she blurted it out. "I wanted to live in New York. I've always loved art history, so I thought being a curator would be so amazing. And I'd be right there with all those museums. I could just pop into the Frick or the Morgan Library."

"So apply for a job there."

"Oh, I have. I've applied to both of those and dozens of others, but I'm sure mine's just one more résumé to add to a very tall pile. Sometimes they send nice rejections. One rejection came in an envelope with an adhesive flap that glowed orange from the cheese puffs some intern was having for lunch. It's the little touches, you know? Makes it classy."

He made a face not unlike the one she'd made at the time. "You're joking, right?"

"I wish I were."

"Don't give up."

Molly was taken aback by what looked very much like sincere confidence in her.

"Someone has to get the job. Why not you?"

She grinned. "From your lips to human resources' ears."

He set down his coffee. "So, you like art museums. Who's your favorite artist?"

"Oh, don't get me started."

"Pick one."

"There's not just one artist, but I love the Pre-Raphaelites. And the Impressionists. I would love to visit the Musée d'Orsay." She rolled her eyes. "Sorry. I get kind of worked up about art. If Renoir were alive, I'd be a stereotypical fangirl." She laughed, but he barely reacted.

"You're not a stereotypical anything I can think of."

"That weird, huh?"

"No." His lips were parted. His eyes locked on hers.

Molly couldn't move. His eyes had green and gold flecks, and his mouth looked like she could kiss it. They drew closer. His lips touched hers, softly at first. Then every emotion she'd been holding back came to the surface and found its way into their kiss.

Outside, a car door closed. Molly flinched and drew back. She couldn't breathe. She could only stare with wide eyes. Zach, looking only slightly less shocked than she, managed to mumble, "Molly."

She shook her head. "This never happened. And it never will."

She fled toward the kitchen. *Have you lost your mind? He's a guest—with a girlfriend. You both are pathetic.*

She didn't make it to the kitchen door before the front door opened. Penelope glared at her then Zach, and Molly's heart sank. She didn't stick around for her mother's entrance.

Penelope walked with her uneven gait to the foot of the stairs and plopped her shopping haul to the floor. "I'll be upstairs." She hobbled up the steps while Zach gathered the bags and followed.

The front door closed, and Liz came into the kitchen. Molly stood at the sink, filling a glass with water. She didn't venture a glance as her mother walked in, but when Liz came to a stop, Molly shut off the water and turned to face her. There was no point in trying to explain.

ZACH CLOSED the door gently and braced himself for Penelope's fury. She sat on the bed with her injured ankle stretched before her. "Don't even try to deny it. I saw you through the window. So did Liz."

Zach was surprised by how quiet and seemingly calm she was. Then she suddenly burst into a torrent of tears. Zach sat down helplessly and watched her sob while he struggled with his own warring emotions. Remorse mixed with relief was the first thing he felt, then the sight and sound of her sobs gripped him with deep, gut-wrenching guilt.

He'd managed to achieve the opposite of what he'd intended. Not only had he not spared her feelings, but he'd broken her heart before Christmas and in a way that was so much worse than a simple breakup. He leaned forward, fighting the urge to go to her. But that would only assuage his own guilt. And he knew her. It would fuel her anger and escalate things. There was nothing he could do now to undo the mess he'd made. He'd hurt Penelope, obviously. And he could only imagine how Molly must feel.

Molly. *She must think I'm a scumbag.* And worse, the worst kind of cheater. Here on vacation with his girlfriend and kissing the innkeeper's daughter. *Who does that?*

The sobbing stopped, and Penelope sat up. Her eyes were dry, but she'd cried off her makeup. The mascara on those linens would never wash out. To her credit, she didn't scream at him. "I hate you, and I want to go home."

Zach nodded. "We can leave in the morning."

"No. I'm leaving tonight. Alone. And I'm taking your car. I'll park it in your parking space and leave the keys with your doorman."

"You can't drive with that boot."

"It's my left foot, and your Porsche is an automatic. I'll be fine."

"Penelope, you're in no condition to drive. You're upset. Get some rest. I can understand your not wanting to travel with me. Take the car, but please wait until you've had some sleep."

Showing no sign of having heard him, she got up, yanked her clothes from the hangers and drawers, and packed in record time. Zach made a few attempts to talk her out of leaving, but when Penelope made up her mind, there was no turning back. She washed her face and, for the first time Zach had ever seen, left without makeup on.

AT DAWN, a taxi pulled into the driveway. Zach left his room key at the desk and started for the train station. He would have an eight-hour train ride to reflect on something he'd rather forget. Penelope had taken the breakup surprisingly well, yet he was no fool. Hell had no fury like Penelope scorned. She would spread the news of what had happened through their whole circle of friends. And the thing was, she didn't need to lie. The truth was enough to exact her revenge. He had it coming—every bit of the gossip and scorn headed his way.

What bothered him even more was what he'd done to Molly. She deserved none of this. He had dragged her into his ugly breakup. But how could he have known that he'd meet her—a woman who'd grown up as he had, in the country, whose life was simple and good. She was kind, smart, and unpretentious. He'd forgotten what it was like to be with someone like her. No, that wasn't true. He had never known anyone like her. If only he'd met her after the breakup. She was the sort of woman he could have fallen in love with if given the chance. But he wouldn't be given the chance, because what he'd done was just foolish. And wrong.

If only he'd done the right thing, which, in retrospect, would have been to break up with Penelope when he first realized their romance was over. He might have come up to Vermont on his own, met Molly, and gone for long walks in the snow. *Zach! Wake up. You're dreaming.* He let out a contemptuous laugh. None of that would have happened. He wouldn't even have bothered to go on the trip. He would have spent the holidays wallowing in misery, in no mood for anyone's company. Then after a week off between Christmas and New Year's, he would have dived right back into the deep end and drowned all his sorrows in work. At least that part of the plan was still intact.

But poor Molly. He'd ruined her Christmas. She must think he did this sort of thing all the time. An irredeemable womanizer. That would be her last impression of him, the opposite of what he thought of her. She was kind and unselfish. She worked hard and asked for so little in return.

Not that she was a saint. He smiled as he thought of her trying to school him in how to cut trees. But even as annoyed or embarrassed as she'd been, she'd shown spirit. She was strong. So strong that she would get over him. He was the one who would need time to get over her. He'd known her for only days, but if he'd had the chance to know her any longer, things could have been different.

Molly Foster, I could have loved you.

SEVEN

"What's that smell?" Will turned from his chair by the fireplace and sniffed.

Molly wrinkled her nose. "Oh! I left eggs on the stove!" She rushed in and found the saucepan of eggs entirely dry, and the eggs were black on the bottom. She took the pan to the sink and ran cold water in it. Then she sank into a chair at the table and buried her face in her hands.

"Molly! What's wrong?" Her mother rushed in, took a look at the pot in the sink, then sat down beside Molly. "So what if the pot's ruined? We'll buy another. There's no need to cry."

Molly lifted her head, pulled a napkin from the holder, and hastily dried her eyes.

Liz stood quietly by while Molly slowly tore the napkin into confetti-sized pieces. *Yay, me! I'm a loser!*

Two days had passed, and neither she nor her mother had mentioned the kiss. Molly had expected a lecture, but there seemed to be an unspoken agreement that Zach would not be mentioned. That suited Molly just fine. Her mother must have known there was nothing to say that Molly wasn't already saying to herself. "I just need some fresh air."

"Fresh air's good." Liz scooped up the shreds of Molly's napkin and said, "We're all set for the weekend wave of guests. Why don't you take the day off? Go shopping. See a movie. Do something fun."

Fun wasn't going to happen for Molly.

Liz refused to give up. "A change of scenery will help."

As miserable as Molly felt, it was still two weeks until Christmas, and she had some shopping to do. "Okay."

Liz got up and gave Molly's shoulders a pat. "Good." Then she went out to the reception room, no doubt to see Will. At least someone had a love life.

DAKOTA SAT down across from Molly. "Hey, listen to this. I got permission to take a long lunch. Don't you love Christmas? Although, I think it's in lieu of a bonus, so yay! And here I go, spending it all in one place." She widened her eyes as if in anticipation. "So?" Her smile faded. "So..." She frowned.

Molly explained what had happened and finished with "I've never done this before." Her shoulders slumped.

"What? Fallen in love? So, you're a slow starter. I didn't learn to smirk till sixth grade, and look at me now."

"It's not love. It was—"

"Lust? It happens."

"No, it was more than that." Molly didn't expect her friend to understand when she barely did.

Dakota gulped a mouthful of cake before speaking. "More than that? Wow! My head, or something else that shall not be named, would have exploded."

"Oh..." Molly searched for the right words to describe it.

"Ovaries! Right! You must be great at *Wheel of Fortune*. Personally, I'd suck at *Jeopardy!* If someone said, 'What are ovaries?' I'd want to answer. Then I'd flash back to our school's fifth-grade sex talk. I'd just moved up from Texas, and I didn't get why the Longhorns' mascot was the female reproductive system. I mean, who wants a giant one of those dancing around the field?"

"Dakota?"

"Right. Sorry. Where were we?"

"Nowhere. With Zach."

Dakota twisted her mouth into what she'd once called its thinking position. "You're not going to want to hear this."

Molly winced.

"But what if he's one of those guys who likes women? All women? Often?"

"That doesn't sound like Zach."

"Just a theory. I've only ever seen the man once."

"Well, he wasn't a flirt."

Dakota finished her coffee. "But he kissed you."

"Yeah." A kiss could mean so many things. At the time, her emotions were close to the surface, while her brain must have been somewhere else. She'd felt a connection with Zach, but how much of that was on her side alone? Had she fallen for the man she'd imagined he was? Was he really someone different, an opportunist slimeball who picked up on her feelings and took advantage of the situation the first chance he got?

Dakota said quietly, "And now he's gone."

"Right again." He was gone. End of story.

Dakota had her compassionate moments. "I'm sorry. I wish I could say something to help."

Molly felt oddly better. "It helped to talk through it."

"I'm glad." Dakota reached over and gripped Molly's hand. "I've gotta go."

Molly nodded as Dakota left, then she stared at her coffee, took a gulp, and headed out to finish her Christmas shopping.

ZACH WALKED INTO A HOLIDAY PARTY, dropped a bottle off with the host, exchanged pleasantries, and was steered toward the drinks and hors d'oeuvres. He got a scotch and went out to the balcony. From a dozen stories up, it was all lights and holiday cheer. Even inside the party, no one seemed to have any problems—at least not that they would discuss. A pretty woman joined him and said the sort of things people said at parties, warm and chatty things he didn't care about. She laughed. Zach smiled back and excused himself. He had made his appearance, and now he would go.

On the way, Carson Attwell, college roommate and former client, put his hand on Zach's shoulder and drew him into a conversation already in full swing. They were talking about how difficult it was to find good employees in the thriving economy. Carson said he'd been looking for an intern—a paid one—to work on a project. Fortunately, the Frick Collection had the cachet to draw a good pool of candidates.

"Carson, may I have a word?" Zach pulled Carson aside. "I know someone you need to see."

On the elevator down to the lobby, he mentally checked off the list of remaining holiday parties he would have to attend. The list had grown shorter upon his return when, out of consideration, a few of his friends had let him know that Penelope would be at their parties. Did he still want to go? It was an easy out for them, and he'd lost his holiday-party spirit. To others, he sent regrets. But the rest of the invitations, from clients and work-related acquaintances, would have to be honored. He'd just weathered one party, and he'd done a good Christmas deed. Only two more parties were left for this week and another the next. After that, he would hole up in his apartment, order in, and wait for the holidays to pass.

EIGHT

Molly was sorting mail at the desk when she let out a squeal. All the guests had checked out, so she didn't hold back. She jumped up and down then reread the letter.

Her mother and Will walked in laughing.

"Mom! I've got an interview at the Frick! I've got a frickin' interview!" She handed the letter to her mother then started to pace. "I'll need an interview outfit. Maybe a suit is too much. Although it's better to overdress than to show up underdressed. I'll need to stay over."

Liz grinned. "Leave that to me. I'll book you a room. When is it?"

"It's... oh my gosh, it's in three days! I've got to go shopping."

Liz looked at Will, whose eyes twinkled. He waved and disappeared.

Liz grabbed her purse and keys. "I'll drive you. You're way too excited to operate heavy equipment."

So they left for a shopping excursion in the village. Although only one interview had been scheduled, Molly's mother urged her to go prepared for a second meeting on the outside chance her prospective employers chose to invite her to another meeting or work-related event while she was in the village. Between visits to clothing and shoe stores, they squeezed in some lunch. By the end of the day, Molly was equipped with all that she needed to make a strong first impression.

Three days later, Molly got off a train at Penn Station and walked out to the street. This was how she'd always dreamed it could be. She would come to Manhattan and nail the interview. Then she would get her dream job and be on her way. Her stomach sank. *But I have to interview first.* She shook off her nerves. *First things first: find the hotel.*

She had looked up the directions and studied the street views online, so she found her hotel with no problem. After unpacking, she booked a ride-hailing service for the morning. Everything would be fine, she kept telling herself.

SHE WAS ready an hour early and, allowing for traffic, had booked a ride uptown that got her there ninety minutes before her interview. She found a nearby diner, where she stared at her phone and sipped a latte until it was time to go. As she walked down the sidewalk, she took deep, even breaths and convinced herself she was ready and this job was hers.

After a short wait, she was met by a thirtyish man who greeted her warmly. "Molly Foster?"

"Yes." She stood and went to shake his hand.

"Carson Attwell."

They joined two others who sat at a conference table, and he introduced them by name and title. Afraid nerves would make her forget the names, she repeated them three times in her head. They talked about Henry Clay Frick and the collection. She'd done her homework, and it had served her well. Leaving the other two on the hiring committee behind, Carson—as he insisted she call him—took her on a tour of the museum and talked about the sort of work she would be doing—if she got the job. She kept reminding herself that it was a big *if*. Thirty minutes later, they found themselves back where they'd started.

Carson smiled. "I can't promise you anything at

this point, of course, but I'm very impressed. We'll let you know either way within the week."

"Thank you. I think this would be an exciting place to work."

"We love your enthusiasm. Zach Moreton was right. He said you'd be perfect."

"*Did he?*" *Hold it together. Just make it out the door.* "Well, thank you so much for taking the time to see me." She extended her hand and managed to gracefully leave. Once outside, she walked numbly. The street numbers were getting lower with each block, so she knew she was headed in the right direction. She walked until her feet hurt, then she hailed a cab and went to her hotel.

Only then did she sink into a chair and let it go—the interview nerves and the shock of finding out this had all been Zach's doing. Was it some afterthought, a gesture of pity, to assuage his guilt? Maybe it was a consolation prize. *You didn't get me, so I'll toss this amazing job at you instead. Why? Because it's nothing for me. It's as easy for me as throwing a table scrap to a stray puppy. Here, girl! Poor you. Have a job. And now leave me alone.*

ON THE TRAIN RIDE HOME, Molly pulled out her phone and sent Carson Attwell an email thanking him for the interview. She explained—well, lied—that since they'd met, she'd been surprised with another offer, which she'd accepted. After more thanks and a gracious closure, she pressed Send. *No, thank you, Zach Moreton.*

The whole incident left her wondering why she had ever wanted the job. It interested her, but it would have come at the cost of her own sense of accomplishment. Once she recovered from the shock of learning that Zach had called in a favor and set up the interview, she tried to convince herself that it was okay. This was how things were done. People did favors. They helped out their friends. And sometimes favors were done for them. But then you owed them, and she didn't want to owe Zach.

As tempting as the job was, she couldn't escape one more glaring fact. She would be taking someone else's job—someone who had worked just as hard to get there —and that didn't sit well with her. If she couldn't get a job on her own, she didn't want it. Some people, Zach included, might call her naïve and idealistic, but she didn't care. She couldn't live with herself if she stole someone else's job.

Then there was the city. She'd always loved the city, or maybe it was only the idea of the city that she loved. She'd barely slept the night before. Even with the windows closed, the traffic noise never let up, and the lights obscured any sense of the natural world. The air was thick with exhaust, and the people were probably great if someone knew them, but she didn't. Was this what she wanted?

At the end of the day, Molly wanted to go home and look up at the stars in the velvety darkness, not streetlights and LED billboards that washed out the vast, beautiful sky. Then there were the trees. On some side streets, trees stood alone in small patches of dirt carved out of the sidewalk, clutching thin plastic bags in their branches.

The city just wasn't for her. But at least she had made the decision, not some human resources manager. She would live life on her terms, and she wouldn't owe a soul for the privilege.

By the time her train pulled into the station, her mind was made up. This was home, and it would continue to be.

ON THE WAY HOME, she told her mother the interview had gone well but that several others were being considered. She was sure the competition was steep, so she wouldn't get her hopes up.

Two days passed before she told her mother—lying again—that she'd gotten an email rejection. The job had been filled, but she felt okay about it. She purposely told her mother the news in Will's presence to keep any ensuing discussion to a minimum. For the most part, it worked. She had used a nonchalant tone, but her mother looked so sympathetic that Molly had averted her eyes to the incoming mail.

The mail was addressed to the inn, so Molly had opened it like she usually did. At first, she thought one of the local Realtors was trying to drum up business, but as she read further, she realized she was looking at a real estate listing.

"Mom, what's this?" She held out the letter.

Liz scanned the page, and her jaw dropped. "Oh, Molly, I didn't want you to find out like this."

"Find out what?" But Molly knew. She just couldn't believe it. "You're selling the farm? And our home?"

"I'm so sorry you found out this way. I was planning to wait until after the holidays."

Molly felt like not only the rug but also the ground had been pulled out beneath her. She wanted to cry out or argue, but all she managed to do was stare at her mom, who was wearing her reassuring *everything's going to be okay* face that she adopted only when everything was inescapably, terribly wrong.

Liz said, "Honey, I've held you back long enough. You missed out on college, and you've given so much to help me and to keep the inn running. Now you can build your own life."

Molly got it. Her mother was doing a good thing, or so she thought. But Molly couldn't help feeling like she'd been kicked out of the nest, and she didn't know how to fly.

Liz seemed surprised by Molly's reaction. "I know it's a shock, but it's not going to happen right away."

Molly gave a stunned nod. Her head might not have been spinning, but her thoughts were. It felt like they would be leaving her father behind. Logically, that made no sense, but sometimes she would look out at the trees all lined up in their rows and think of the times she'd helped her father plant them. Of course, he was gone. She'd had years to recover. But sometimes she would hear a noise, or someone would round the corner, and it would feel perfectly natural for him to just walk through the door. If they left the inn, that would never happen again.

"Are you concerned about your job not panning out? That was only your first interview. There'll be others. Until then, you will have a home. It just might not be here."

"This is my home. I've decided to stay. Or I had, anyway."

It was Liz's turn to be stunned. "I didn't know."

"I was going to tell you. I thought you'd be happy."

Molly had not forgotten that Will was there, watching their back-and-forth as if it were a sad tennis match. "Will, I'm sorry. You shouldn't have to endure discussion of our family issues."

He looked at Liz, but she averted her eyes. Watching the two, Molly decided poor Will just wasn't picking up the cue. This was his chance to leave. As much as she liked him, this was none of his business.

Will didn't appear to agree. "The reason this is happening now—"

"Will." Liz shook her head, but he ignored her and continued.

"Sorry, Liz. There's no good time to say it, but it has to be said. I'm going to Florida, and I've asked your mother to come with me."

"A vacation? Together?" That was just weird. First her mother was selling the tree farm, and now she and Will were planning vacations together. *What's happening?*

When Will went over and slipped his hand into Liz's, she looked uncomfortable. That made two of them, because Molly wasn't exactly enjoying the discussion. So her mother and Will were a thing. Molly tried not to wrinkle her face. It wasn't like she hadn't suspected Will's feelings, but it looked like her mother shared them. That was something Molly would need time to digest. In the meantime, this hand-holding was over the top.

Will cleared his throat.

Molly had never seen him look so awkward. Ordinarily, Will was the strong, silent type, very laid back.

He said, "Molly, it's not a vacation. We're moving there permanently."

"What?" It felt like one of those math word problems where everything sounded like English, but nothing made sense. *If Will leaves for Florida, driving fifty-five miles an hour, and I kidnap my mother and make a run for the border, who will need to find a rest stop first?* "You're shacking up with my mother?"

"I wouldn't put it that way. I love her." He put his arm around Liz's shoulder.

"But not enough to marry her." *Wow. When did I turn into my mother? Except not, because all I did was kiss a guy. She's moving in with a guy that she barely... well, okay, she's known him since high school, and now she'll know him a lot better. She probably already does. Ew! Stop thinking. It'll only get worse.*

If Will hadn't been such a good family friend, Molly would have been seriously tempted to throw him out of the inn. She wasn't sure how, since Will was six foot three and in pretty good shape for his age. But she would be empowered by her mounting adrenaline-infused annoyance.

He said, "We're taking things one step at a time."

Molly muttered. "But just not in order." Then she looked at her mother directly. "Am I the only adult in the room?"

Liz cast a cautioning look at Will then said to Molly, "I know this is a lot to take in."

"Yeah, I need time to reflect." *Or throw up.* "Excuse me." She left the two lovebirds alone and escaped to her room.

NINE

Zach sat at the end of the bar at his favorite midtown Irish pub. With its walls of dark wood, soft lighting, and tucked-away booths lining the wall across from the bar, the place was a respite from the New York side street that, with one step, transported patrons to another place and time. For some, it was a reminder of the Ireland of their ancestors and genetic memories. For Zach, it was a place to wallow in self-loathing.

Zach stared into his beer. *How long has it been, nearly two weeks?* He counted the days. No, eleven. It seemed like forever since he'd seen Molly Foster. Her name alone made his heart sink. Was it love? He'd never had a chance to find out. But he knew she was different, and what he felt for her was different from anything he'd known before.

For eleven days, he'd relentlessly relived the most regrettable events of his life. He knew he was to blame. No one would argue that point. But he couldn't understand how he'd managed to give his emotions free rein. He'd always prided himself on his skill at reading people and reacting with measured thought and good sense. That was the man who went up to Vermont. But the man who kissed Molly and went back to New York had lost his mind. And his heart.

Even if no one had seen their fateful kiss, it couldn't have led to anything positive. He was there with his girlfriend. It didn't matter that he was planning to break up with her later. He was with her then. So to try to begin a relationship with Molly under such circumstances was not only unfair to Molly but, of course, to Penelope as well.

Then there was Molly's mother. She had opened her inn—her home—to him. And what had he done? She would never forgive him.

Molly. He sighed. What had he expected her to do, sneak around behind Penelope's back? Nothing could've come of it. And now nothing would.

Zach had gone over this so many times that he wondered why he even bothered. *What was I thinking?* The answer ached in his heart. He hadn't been thinking at all. And he missed Molly so profoundly that he knew his regret was a scar that would not go away.

His phone buzzed, a welcome distraction. He glanced at the text. Carson had been detained in the office, but he'd managed to escape and was one block away. Zach had been so lost in thought that he'd barely noticed the time.

While he waited, Zach glanced at his email. A new listing drew his attention—a farm. It brought to mind how good he'd felt working at the Christmas tree farm. Growing up, he'd never known any other life, so he had always dreamed of a glamorous life in the city. When he moved to New York and made his dream happen, he'd put his old life so far behind him that he'd nearly forgotten the satisfaction of honest, physical work. There was no having to maneuver his way through a minefield of hidden motives, mistrust, and schemes. The tree farm had awakened a nagging dissatisfaction that he was only beginning to fully realize. He found himself longing for a simpler life, a life he would never have—at least not with Molly.

"You look brimming with holiday spirit!"

Zach looked up toward the familiar voice. "Attwell!" He extended his hand, and Carson sat down for their annual holiday cocktail. They'd been out of college for enough years that Zach now had to count.

Seven years. Look at them. The college roommates had done well for themselves.

Carson sat down and ordered a beer, and they chatted about family and friends they both knew. Carson would head to the airport the next morning, while Zach would drive upstate to his mother's. They laughed their way through a round then ordered another.

When they arrived at a conversational lull, which was rare for them, Carson leaned back with a satisfied look. "Oh, by the way, your friend Molly Foster was fantastic."

Hearing her name made Zach's heart sink, but he recovered enough to force out a reply. "Really? That's great. So you're hiring her?"

Carson shrugged. "We were ready to make her an offer as soon as she left, but before we could, she emailed that she'd had another offer. The same day."

That sounded unlikely. There had to be more to the story. "So the Attwell allure failed to charm her."

"I guess. She seemed really eager, but..." Carson paused and reflected. "You know, I think things shifted when I mentioned your name. Maybe it's your charm that failed." Carson laughed then frowned when he saw Zach's reaction. "Did I touch a raw nerve?"

"Yeah, maybe."

"So, I'm guessing Molly is not just a friend."

"Oh, she's that and so much less. Just ask her. She holds me in such low esteem that she's given up her dream job out of loathing for me."

Carson set down his beer. "And you thought getting her an interview might win you some points?"

Zach nearly laughed. "Not a chance. It was already dead in the water."

"Then why—"

"I just wanted to help her."

Carson flagged down the bartender and ordered a couple of Irish whiskeys. "We need something stronger if we're going to deep dive into this."

It didn't take long for Zach to give Carson a clear understanding of what had gone on in Vermont.

Carson shook his head. "This is so un-Zach-like. I'm actually kind of impressed."

"Don't be."

Carson leaned his arm on the bar. "So, let me get this straight, you were sleeping upstairs with your girlfriend while trying to gain ground with Molly downstairs by the fire?"

Zach was back in his loop of reliving and loathing himself. "It didn't start out that way. And in my defense, I'd been planning to break up with Penelope since October."

Carson shook his head. "I could have told you she wasn't your type."

"Yeah, I know. But what kind of a weasel breaks up over the holidays? By the time she recovered from surgery, it was too late. I was stuck for the rest of the holiday season."

Carson's eyes narrowed. "Sorry. I'm still stuck on the image of you in your room with your girlfriend, doing the horizontal mambo in an old inn with the rickety wooden floors squeaking in rhythm, while—"

Zach held up a palm. "Let me stop you right there. The first night, I was exhausted from driving."

Carson leaned back with a skeptical smirk.

Zach ignored him. "Then when Penelope fell and got a concussion—"

"Pushed her down the stairs, did you?" Carson's eyes twinkled.

"No! Attwell, what kind of—"

"I'm kidding! Wow. Aren't you the sensitive one?"

Zach leveled a wry look at him. "On our way to go skiing, while checking her makeup, she slipped in the lobby and fell in the fountain."

Zach had to wait for Carson to stop laughing before he could finish the story. When he finally did, Carson said, "If anyone can injure herself doing makeup, Penelope can."

"She had a mild concussion. After that, she was afraid sex might injure her brain."

Carson slammed down his glass and gripped Zach's arm. After he swallowed, he said, "Please don't do that again. I almost sprayed triple-distilled Irish whiskey all over the bar guns. Now, where did she get an idea like that?"

Zach was feeling increasingly uncomfortable. "I had no interest in her by then, but she asked the doctor."

"And he said that? Maybe you need a new doctor. Of course, I forgot you didn't have much of a choice up there with the mountain folk."

"Vermont. No, but the doctor happened to mention that studies suggest sex could affect recovery time, but he was talking about gender."

Carson folded his arms. "This gets better and better."

"He meant women recover faster than men. But you know, Penelope's attention span doesn't always make it to the end of a sentence, so her takeaway was that sex would injure her brain."

Carson's face was blank except for the glint in his eyes.

Zach wasn't amused. "After that, all bets were off, which was perfect. I was just going through the motions. Not those motions." Zach shut his eyes, but he could still hear Carson snickering. "In my mind, it was already over. And then I met Molly, and I just wanted to get through the holidays and maybe go back to Vermont and see if... maybe..."

Carson leaned back with a philosophical look on his face. "Back up a minute. So, you'd decided to break up then planned a dirty weekend together—"

Zach interrupted. "Penelope did. Weeks ahead."

"That'll teach you to plan."

Zach couldn't disagree.

Carson continued. "So you went away, to *not* have sex, and you fell in love with the innkeeper's daughter, who hates you."

"I never said love."

"No, but I know you. It was implied."

Zach stared at the contents of his glass. "I thought I was being sort of noble to Penelope, sparing her feelings. But she'd have been better off if I'd dumped her. We all would."

Carson lifted his eyebrows. "For what it's worth, she's recovered. I've seen her at two holiday parties with some new guy, a personal trainer. He's got a line of testosterone-boosting supplements he sells in infomercials, which makes him a celebrity in her eyes. Yeah, the two of them were all over each other's comfort and joy." Carson raised an eyebrow.

"Heartbroken, was she?" Zach smirked.

"Yeah, something like that."

Carson finished his drink and looked at his watch. "Look. Closing words of advice."

"Did I ask for advice?"

"No, but it's the season of giving, so here's my gift to you."

Zach winced in anticipation.

"You screwed up."

"Don't sugarcoat it, Carson."

"And your timing sucks."

"I'm feeling the holiday spirit already." Zach rubbed his hand over his face.

"But Molly's amazing."

"Yeah."

Carson's phone alarm buzzed, and he stood and signaled the bartender. "Sorry, I've got a thing to go to."

They argued over the tab, but Carson was too quick on the draw with his credit card. He turned to Zach. "Just do one thing for me."

"Sure, what?"

"Do whatever you have to, but fix it."

"Yeah, no problem."

Carson gripped Zach's shoulder. "I mean it. Do it, or you'll regret it for the rest of your life."

"Okay, Bogie. Merry Christmas to you too!"

Carson grinned and wished him the same and walked out into the drizzling twilight.

Zach remained in his seat, not quite ready to go. He checked his email and messages and returned to the real estate listings he'd been perusing when Carson arrived. "Fix it," he muttered as he reopened the browser tab.

"Maybe I can."

TEN

Liz and Will sat down at the kitchen table. "So that went well." Liz leaned back in her chair.

Will stretched his legs out. "Look, I know you're not happy, but there's no good time for something like that."

Liz stared at her hands. She'd grown used to making her own decisions, and this didn't sit well with her. "Maybe, but you might have let me in on the plan."

"There was no plan. There was an opportunity, and I seized it."

Liz nodded. That was so Will—all action, no thought of the consequences. But wasn't that what had attracted her to him? He was past fifty, but he hadn't let himself grow old and staid. He didn't worry about consequences. That wasn't always a good thing, but the flip side was that he still had a spirit of adventure. She loved that about him.

"A breakup's a breakup. They hurt. But hanging on through the holidays just made it worse. Sometimes, you just gotta pull off the bandage."

Liz wrinkled her nose. "So you're likening Molly's leaving her home to an adhesive bandage?"

Will's eyes drew together. "There's no winning this, is there?"

"Not really, no."

Will leaned closer. "Sorry, Lizzie."

Her gaze softened. "Maybe it would have been just as hard no matter when I told her. But I'm used to deciding these things."

"Yeah, I know. She's your daughter. And I barged in without thinking. Sorry."

Will reached over the table and took her hand in both of his. "As for shacking up, maybe I'm just waiting for the right time."

At the same moment, the realization of what he'd just said clearly struck them both.

Liz lifted an eyebrow. "So timing doesn't matter... except when it does?"

His eyes sparkled as he glanced toward the door. "I just thought of something I need to do at the farm."

Liz took pleasure in making him squirm. "Oh, really? What's that?"

"I don't know, but I'll think of something." He paused long enough to kiss her on the forehead.

As he went to the door, she called after him. "I'm in no hurry, but if you happen to notice an adhesive bandage on my left ring finger, you'll know that the timing is right."

Will grinned. "Good to know."

MOLLY FINISHED CHECKING in the last guest for the day. All of their regular guests had arrived and were making themselves at home in their rooms, by the fire, or taking walks in the winter wonderland. Molly's favorite Christmas carols were playing, and the inn smelled of cinnamon and cloves, which Liz mixed with water and left simmering in a slow cooker. A wooden crate of ornaments sat by the tree so guests could hang an ornament or two if they felt in the spirit. The continental breakfast array had transitioned to a Christmas cookie station with frosting at the ready for decorating. And Molly was at the desk, chin in her hands, looking glum.

Liz came in from the kitchen. "Dishes are done, and all's well with the world. Why don't we go for a walk?"

Molly lifted her eyes. "Don't bother. It won't cheer

me up." All the Christmas cheer around her was having the opposite effect.

"I'm not asking. Here." She set Molly's coat on her lap. "Put it on."

This was out of character. Liz wasn't demanding by nature, so her command threw Molly off enough that she didn't even bother to resist. They went outside and followed the walking path Will kept clear for guests. It went into the woods and wound through the trees before working its way back to the inn. When they were far beyond earshot of guests, Liz said, "I've been thinking."

Molly still hadn't recovered from having her mother's new life plan with Will sprung on her, so she wasn't sure she wanted to hear what her mother had been thinking. She braced herself.

"I'm keeping the inn."

That was unexpected. Molly didn't know what to say.

"But I'm still selling the farm."

Molly's eyebrows drew together.

Liz touched Molly's arm. "Hear me out. I need the sale to help fund my retirement. I've saved over the years, but it's not quite enough. And medical costs are a big question mark. You never know..."

Yeah. I learned that one the hard way when Dad

died. Thanks for the reminder. Then a thought gripped her. "Mom, are you okay?"

Liz put her arm around Molly's shoulders. "Yes, honey. I'm fine."

Molly started breathing again.

"But it makes sense to keep the inn. And I want you to run it. Since you'll be neighbors with whoever buys the Christmas tree farm, I want you to approve of the buyer."

Molly laughed. "So I can't gripe at you when I hate them?"

"No, because you might want to pool your resources for marketing purposes and because I want us to be business partners. We'll work out all the details, but basically, you'll get to stay like you want, and I'll have someplace to stay when I come up to visit. And someday, the inn will be yours."

Molly didn't like what that implied, but she brushed the thought aside. Not only would she be able to stay on at the inn, but she would also be able to run it. She threw her arms about her mother's neck. "Thank you! I won't disappoint you."

"I know that." Liz slipped her arm about Molly's waist, and they continued along the path. "I would have done this in the first place, but I honestly thought that you wanted to leave."

"I know." Molly looked at the inn and the farm beyond it. "I guess things have changed. I didn't see it coming, but I want different things than I once thought I did."

"That's part of life."

"I guess so." Molly walked arm in arm with her mother and felt like her life had fallen into place. It was one of those moments that came too seldom, where life was in balance. Losing her father had taught her to value rare moments like these. Her heart had been wounded, but now she could pour her heart into the inn.

"Mom, thank you."

MOLLY AND DAKOTA sat on the floor in Molly's room, wrapping presents while their favorite Christmas movie played on Molly's computer.

Dakota eyed her glum friend then caught sight of Santa on the screen. In a low, bellowing voice, she said, "Ho, ho, ho, Molly! What would you like Santa to bring you for Christmas?"

"Good try, Santa. But you know you can't bring me what I want."

"Well, no, Molly. We had this talk last year, remember? Santa can't bring you a smokin' hot stud."

Molly looked up and laughed in spite of herself.

Obviously encouraged, Dakota continued acting as Santa. "Besides, you think I pulled that Vermont inn out of my chimney? No, those things are hard to come by. But I did it for you 'cause you're on my good list."

"Thanks, Santa," Molly said wryly.

Dakota's Santa dug through one of the shopping bags. "But if that inn's not enough, Santa might have something inflatable in here."

Molly held out her palm. "That's okay, Santa. I'm good."

"Yes you are, little Molly."

Sometimes, Dakota didn't know when to stop. She went on in her Santa voice, "Now where did I put that big lump of coal from Santa's backyard grill? The one that's as big as that scumbucket's little black car?"

"Dakota?"

"Yes?" Apparently realizing she'd used her Santa voice, she went back to her own. "I mean, yes?"

"We don't need to speak of him ever again."

Dakota nodded obediently. "Would you hand me that Zach? I mean sack. I swear I didn't mean to do that." She looked down and got busy taping wrapping paper in place.

Molly threw her hands in the air. "Okay, I give up! Zach, Zach, Zach, Zach! There, I said it."

"A lot," Dakota muttered.

"For some reason, not because he deserves it, I can't stop thinking about him."

"Give it some time."

"How much time? Do we have any hard numbers on that?"

A car door slammed, so Molly got up to look out the window. She'd checked in the last guest, but people sometimes showed up without reservations. It was her mother and Will, laughing and pulling shopping bags from Will's truck. Her mom looked really happy.

Will had whisked Liz off for an afternoon away from the inn. It was good for her. She didn't do enough for herself, but Will did. Maybe they weren't all that bad for each other. In the past year or two, she had wondered if her mother would ever find someone again. No one could replace her father, but her mother deserved to be happy. And if being with Will did that for her, she deserved it. As Molly watched them, she realized her mother could do far worse than Will. He was tall and rugged. Not bad for his fifties. He must have been handsome back in the day. Liz looked at him and grinned. He made her mom happy. Molly smiled to herself and went back to her wrapping.

ELEVEN

Zach hurriedly packed a bag while he spoke with the phone set on speaker. "Mom, something's come up."

"But you'll be here for Christmas."

"Yes. I just need to take care of something, so I might not get there until Christmas Day."

"All right, honey. Be safe."

Zach smiled. "Okay, Mom. Love you."

"I love you, too."

He finished packing and opened his computer. The inn had an online reservation system, which meant Zach could book a room without talking to anyone. That part was crucial, since neither Molly nor her mother would be eager to see him. In what felt like a Christmas miracle, there was one room left for the week, and he took it. He'd had a few drinks with Carson, so he wouldn't drive until morning. His office was closed until after the new year. That gave him a little over a week, minus Christmas Day at home in central New York. One week to convince Molly to love him.

"Zach?"

He'd expected Molly's mother to hang up on him, so he took this as a positive sign. She was still on the phone, but she wasn't chastising him. Yet. But he could hear the restraint in her voice. "Liz, I know I made a thorough mess of everything, but would you please let me explain?"

He'd never experienced such a long, painful three seconds.

"We're pretty busy around here with the holidays," she said.

"I know. But I'm here in town—"

"Here? Why?"

"I was hoping you could carve out some time to meet with me."

"Oh? Why?" It wasn't really a question. It was more of a no.

Zach would not be deterred. "And we need to meet alone. Away from the inn."

"You mean to talk about Molly."

"I do."

"I don't really want to run interference for you."

"Please. It's important."

Liz was a remarkable person. He knew this because she had agreed, albeit reluctantly, to meet with him. Few mothers would have agreed to do so under the circumstances. But she did, and he chalked it up to her Christmas goodwill.

She was as eager to spare Molly's feelings as he was, so she suggested a local hangout in the next town over, where the coffee was strong, the menu was laden with gluten and meat, and the clientele was crusty. But the chances of Molly showing up there were almost zero, so that made it perfect.

Zach arrived first and found a table in the corner, where he could keep an eye on the door. If for some reason Molly showed up and surprised them, he had an escape route. There were no men's or women's rooms, just one bathroom with a sign on the door that said Head. Beyond that was a back door where he could duck out unseen.

Liz arrived as the server was walking away. Zach said, "I hope you don't mind, but I ordered two coffees.

I remembered you take yours with cream and no sugar."

"Thank you." She took her coat off and draped it over the chair beside hers. "That's the thing about you that I don't understand. You're so thoughtful about some things."

She didn't say it, but there was a definite *but* at the end of her sentence. To Liz's credit, she listened. He explained what had led up to the ill-fated kiss and how breaking up with Penelope over the holidays had seemed cruel. And yes, he now realized he'd made a mistake.

Liz was direct. "But you made that mistake with my daughter."

"I don't take any of this lightly, especially Molly."

"You're very good at saying all the right things. I just wish you were as good at doing the right thing."

"That's why I'm here."

Liz shook her head, and Zach thought she might leave, but she didn't. She asked a lot of questions, and he answered them. It wasn't always easy or comfortable, but he owed her answers. If he had any hope of reaching Molly, he would need Liz's forgiveness.

Liz stared into her coffee and frowned. "But you went away on vacation with someone you were going to break up with?"

"She had booked it to surprise me. There was no way out of it without telling her it was over."

Liz almost looked understanding, at least for a second or two, then she looked him straight in the eye. "Maybe you should have."

He nodded. He imagined, from her point of view, he must look like a scumbag. Heck, he even looked like that from his point of view.

From the look on her face, he could see she was mulling something over. She finally said, "I'm sorry, but I can't get over the fact that you were still with your girlfriend, staying in the same room together."

At least she was more discreet about discussing it than Carson had been.

She continued. "And you divided your time between the woman in your room and my daughter. That's what I just... can't..." She shook her head and looked away.

Zach shut his eyes and mustered the courage, if not the words, for what he had to say next. "Liz. We weren't... together... like that..." *I cannot be having this conversation.*

Liz stared with no expression except for her narrow eyes peering at him. He couldn't blame her. He wouldn't buy his story either.

So it was time to man up and accept the bitter consequences of his actions because there was nothing else he could say or do short of getting down on his knees to grovel and whimper. And he wasn't above doing that if he thought it would do him any good, but it wouldn't. He'd laid all his cards on the table.

Except for the last one. "If I were you, I would hate me. Given that, what I'm going to say might shock you."

"Oh, I don't see how you could any more."

She glanced toward the door. He could see it coming. She was seconds from leaving unless he said something to stop her. "I want to buy the Christmas tree farm."

That worked. Not only did that stop her from leaving, but from the look on her face, he might have caused some sort of health episode. "Liz?"

She looked frankly at him. "Is everything just a business deal for you?"

"No! That's not what this is. I want to live here and —" Then he just blurted it out. "I'm falling in love with her."

"Molly?"

"Yes." Of course, Molly! Who else? What the heck?

Liz was apparently speechless. But she managed to look so sorry for him that he had to say something, if only to ease his discomfort. "I know that I've hurt her."

"You hurt her a lot."

That made him feel physically ill. He could take all the scorn. He deserved it. But hearing her describe what he had done to Molly was a harsh blow.

Liz said, "Because from my perspective, it looked like she was falling in love, too."

Zach was stunned. And thrilled. He could have reached over the table and hugged and kissed Liz, but he didn't. *Talk about the wrong thing to do.* But he wanted to ask her to say those words again. And again.

Liz shook her head. "I'm not sure why, but I've actually stopped wanting to punch you in the face."

"Thanks. That means a lot to me." He meant it.

"As it should." She exhaled, shaking her head. "But honestly, Zach. Couldn't you have broken up with your girlfriend, maybe taken her home first, before you kissed Molly? I mean, New York's just a day's ride away. Or a flight, if you're that impatient. Which you apparently are."

He nodded. "You're right. I was wrong, and I'm sorry. I didn't plan it. It just happened. I have no defense except love makes people stupid."

She wrinkled her face skeptically. "So I've heard. But I've never seen such an extreme example." A light came to her eyes, then she smiled while she shook her head slowly and sighed. "It's up to Molly."

Zach felt something he thought he'd lost two weeks before. It was hope—just a sliver but more than he'd left home with. "Really?"

"Don't look so happy. I've taken the property off the market to revise the listing. I'm selling the farm on its own. Molly wants to stay here, so I'm keeping the inn, and she'll manage it for me. She'll have to live next door to the new owner, and it's in both their best interests to coordinate their marketing efforts. So since she'll have to work with him or her, she'll have to approve of the buyer. Honestly, Zach, I wouldn't count on it. But for some reason, I believe you. And I might even forgive you. Someday."

"Okay."

"How long are you in town for?"

"Until New Year's Day. I, uh, booked a room at the inn."

She eyed him for a long moment. "Okay, I'll give you the week to convince her."

"I'll do it." *But how?*

Liz put her hands on the table, leaned toward him, and quietly said, "But understand this. I might look nice and mild-mannered, but I am a mother in every sense of the word. And if you hurt my Molly again, I will personally, and with pleasure, see to it that you're singing first soprano in the next *Messiah* sing-along. Understood?"

"Yes, ma'am."

"Merry Christmas." With a sweet smile and what looked like a self-satisfied nod, Liz walked out to her car.

TWELVE

MOLLY COLLAPSED on her bed and stared at the ceiling. She didn't need a man to be happy, but she'd felt something for Zach. She still did. She wondered how she had managed that in such a short time. From the first moment she saw him, she'd felt it. Like two chemistry students with poor listening skills, she and Zach had caused an explosion. She couldn't speak for him, but her feelings must have been simmering close to the surface for that kiss to have happened. Without saying a word, they both knew something was there. All it took was a moment alone, close enough for them to lean in. Maybe they both knew that the kiss was going to happen. It had only been a matter of time.

Molly sat up. *Oh my gosh. I'm as guilty as he is.* She'd been blaming him, but she'd been just as responsible. She knew his situation. It wasn't like he'd forced her. He hadn't. All he did was look into her eyes. She took in a sharp breath. *I kissed him!*

On the list of regrets she would try not to remember for the rest of her life, this would be close to the top. She knew she couldn't think when she was around him. She should never have gotten so close to him, especially when they were alone. But she'd wanted that kiss. She had been just as wrong, at least as far as their kiss was concerned.

As Molly buried herself up to her neck in guilt, a thought occurred to her. What if he knew he was charming and had honed his technique so well that he could go anywhere, girlfriend or not, and do this on every vacation, this time to her? Some guys were like that. And they were called jerks. Molly despised jerks. And she would despise Zach.

Eventually.

The motion detector dinged, signaling that a guest had come through the front door. Liz went out to the front desk and stopped when she saw it was Zach. She glanced over her glasses. "She's in her room. I assume you have her number, so I'll let you call her and tell her you're here. I'm not getting in the middle of this."

He nodded. He'd already made this awkward enough. There was no need to drag Liz any further into his misery. Once in his room, he dropped his bag on the luggage rack, pulled out his phone, and dialed Molly. It rang, but she didn't pick up. He tried again. No answer. Unless she'd lost her phone, she was ignoring his calls. Leaving a voicemail message was not going to work. He went to the window and gazed out at the snow-covered lawn. He wasn't going to find her in here.

Molly's room was in a residential wing of the inn. He could wait in the reception area until Molly emerged from her fortress of solitude. But while he waited, he doubted Liz would want him draped over the furniture while she was trying to work. He was lucky she'd even let him get this far. He'd best not push his luck.

He headed outside. Walking always helped clear his head, and this was a good time to acquaint himself with the property he hoped to buy. He walked over to the farm. Will was busy with a line of customers, but he glanced over at Zach, unsurprised. Liz must have told Will he was here. Zach's preference would have been to walk around the property to get a sense of its scope, but Will looked like he could use a hand. So Zach offered, and Will put him to work outside, helping customers.

Zach was used to selling real estate, but Christmas trees were different. The people who came here were happy. They weren't just taking home trees. They were bringing Christmas spirit into their homes, and it all began here. Christmas trees brought families together and reminded them of the joy of giving. Zach hadn't seen one judgmental or jaded person here, yet that described most of his real estate customers. He stopped and scanned the acres of trees then looked back at the shop. This was where he belonged. He was certain of it. Now he just needed Molly to see it.

A single mom with three kids asked for some help. When the youngest complained that she couldn't see anything, he checked with the mom for permission, then lifted the little girl onto his shoulders. Soon, she spotted her favorite tree, and the family agreed. Five minutes later, Zach hoisted the tree over his shoulder and was walking them to the front when Molly emerged from the gift shop and nearly ran into him. He could read almost every emotion that came over her face—none of them good—and saw the restraint she was forced to show when she realized he had customers with him. Without saying a word, she turned and walked away.

The tree was paid for, baled, and tied onto the roof of the car in record time. Zach waved as the family drove off, then he scanned the property for Molly. She might have returned to the inn to avoid a confrontation. But he thought it unlikely, given the steam coming out of her ears—well, almost. She was angry, but he'd expected that. The hardest thing to take was the pain in her eyes. Seeing that was as bad as a punch to the gut.

When he'd convinced himself that she wasn't outside, he ducked inside. The line was gone, and he approached Will. "If you're caught up, I've got something I need to take care of."

"She's outside," Will said.

Zach took one look at Will's knowing expression and thought better of trying to deny that his task had anything to do with Molly.

"She was heading that way." Will tilted his head toward the back of the barn.

"Thanks, Will." Zach turned to leave.

"Don't thank me yet." With a wry smile, Will folded his arms and leaned back on the counter.

THIRTEEN

ZACH ROUNDED the corner and found Molly where Will had said she would be.

"I don't want a scene. Where's your car?" she asked.

Zach had thought through a dozen scenarios on his drive up to Vermont, but this wasn't one of them. His confusion must have shown on his face. "It's Christmastime. No one wants to come here and find us arguing."

"I wasn't planning to argue."

Molly walked away, and he followed. When she arrived at the parking lot, she stopped abruptly. "Where is it?"

The last thing on his mind was his car. "Oh, that. I sold it to a friend. I needed something more practical." He led her to a pickup. She eyed it then looked at him, her eyes full of doubt. They got in. As Zach pulled out of the driveway, Molly gave him directions to an out-of-the-way bar on a hill overlooking the valley. When they arrived, Molly led the way inside, and they settled into a vinyl-upholstered booth in the corner. Molly couldn't have chosen a better place for a private conversation. It wasn't a nice place, and he wasn't ready to call it clean, but he felt sure no one would bother them here.

The place was dimly lit by illuminated beer signs, and Zach doubted any part of it had been updated since before he was born, including the light bulb that was out near the small restroom alcove. They had, however, made an effort to decorate for the holidays. Behind the bar, varied lengths of crumpled metallic Mylar garland were haphazardly draped over the framed beer-ad mirrors.

As if reading his mind, Molly said, "This seemed like a good place to meet where we wouldn't be overheard."

Zach's eyes widened as he nodded. "Good job with that. I don't expect this place gets all that much business."

Judging from the characters perched at the bar, Zach had no doubt their presence, whether they were overheard or not, wouldn't be remembered.

The bartender came over and took their drink order. Unwilling to wager his intestinal health on how recently they'd cleaned the tap lines, Zach ordered a bottle of beer. Molly opted for a glass of chardonnay. It was all Zach could do to resist an "Excellent choice, madam" as the bartender returned to the bar.

"Well?" Molly looked anything but receptive.

This wasn't exactly the scene he had pictured when he'd imagined declaring his undying love. Nothing he said here could make anything better between them. Maybe taking him here was Molly's way of ensuring that. Very efficient. Nothing romantic could transpire. Zach braced himself and forged onward. "I made a mistake. I admit it. And I'm sorry."

Molly stared blankly. "We should have come in separate cars."

That seemed awfully harsh when he'd barely begun. The gentlemanly thing to do would be to offer to take her home. If he did, he wouldn't get another chance to talk to her like this. After everything he had done to get here, he couldn't believe his trip was meant to be over so quickly. Her actions stung, but he got the words out. "I can take you home if you'd like."

Upon hearing that, she seemed to relax, and a lost look came into her eyes. That disturbed Zach. *Has she felt threatened up to this point?* But she'd asked him to drive her somewhere in the first place, so that couldn't be it.

The bartender set their drinks on the table and

said, "Couldn't help but overhear. If you need a ride, I can call one of the boys."

Molly smiled. "It's okay. I'm fine."

He lingered, unconvinced.

"Thanks, Hal." Her face brightened, and the bartender left. She explained, "I went to school with his sons."

Zach nodded. *If they're anything like their dad, that must have made for some fascinating class discussions.* But as he spoke, he had a sudden vision of "the boys" looking like linebackers spoiling for a fight, just for sport.

Molly said, "I don't know whether I want to walk away, tell you off, or just punch you."

Zach didn't doubt he deserved it. "You could do all three, although probably not in that order." The flash of fire in her expression didn't bode well for him. "Or... whatever you want."

"I'm not some naïve, small-town girl. Guests have made passes before."

"You think that's what it was, just a pass?" She looked at him as if he had planned it, like he was one of those guys who harassed women and called it flirting. "So you must think I'm some sort of—"

"Flirt? Cheater? Womanizer? I don't know what you are. I've been trying to figure that out."

Zach said, "I had one girlfriend in high school. She

broke up with me during our first semester of college apart. I had another girlfriend my junior year in college. She was a senior. She graduated and married some guy she worked with. I've gone out with some women, but it's never been serious. Penelope and I were together, if that's what you could call it, for six months. She's already got someone new."

"What a lovely story."

Zach rolled his eyes and leaned back. "Look, I get that you hate me, but bitterness doesn't become you."

"I don't care what becomes me." Her eyes narrowed, but he thought he saw more hurt than hate there. It was enough to encourage him to go on.

"My point is I'm not one of those guys. I wish I could go back in time, break up with Penelope just before her appendix ruptured, and then come up here alone and meet you. That would have made for a much better story, but I—" He stopped. This was getting him nowhere. *What does she want from me?* "Look, if I thought I wouldn't stick to the floor, I would get down on both knees and grovel. Which would make it the second time, both on the same day. The first was—"

"My mother? She told me." The corner of her mouth twitched, and she practically smiled. Perhaps that was progress.

"I felt something between us that I've never felt before."

She met his eyes directly. "Feelings aren't always enough."

"But you felt it, too."

"I didn't say that." But she didn't deny it was true.

There was something there. He was sure of it. But she didn't want to give in to her feelings, and he couldn't blame her. She'd convinced herself that he was a serial womanizer who had tried to add one more notch to his belt. Anything he might say to refute it only fed her doubt. Seeing her had nearly convinced him that he would never redeem himself in her eyes. Years from now, he would look back with no less bitter regret than he felt at this moment. He could see the situation was hopeless. He would have to take her home, make a hotel reservation online, then stop for the night on his way home.

She stared at her glass. "You hurt me." She lifted her eyes and glared. "No one does that to me more than once."

That was it. She was through with him. Yet even in the face of her contempt, he wasn't through with her. Not yet. "I will never hurt you again."

She laughed. It was unexpected and biting. "No one can say that. I'm sure my father thought he would never hurt my mother or me, but he did when he left us. Sometimes it just happens in spite of it all."

A wave of pain struck him as he realized she was

right. He would hurt her again—with or without meaning or wanting to—simply because that was a part of life that couldn't be avoided. But as he fought the urge to take her into his arms, as if that would convince her, he knew he would hold her and do all he could to shield her from pain for the rest of his life, if she would let him. But if she wouldn't, it would be the true test of his love, because he would have to let go.

"Molly."

She tilted her head back as though nothing he said could change anything. He reminded himself that her bitterness was only a mask for pain.

He said, "When I spoke to your mother—"

She laughed. "Why was that again? To ask for my hand?"

"No, your farm."

The bitter mask was suddenly gone. "Why?"

He looked at her gently. "We're not all that different, you know. I was mistaken about what I wanted in life. I thought leaving farm life for the city—bright lights, fancy car—would be exciting, which it was. But it didn't make me happy. I think I knew all along something was missing, but I didn't know until I came here what it was."

"Christmas trees? That's what was missing? Wow. Talk about Christmas spirit! Someone's had a little too much Christmas party punch." She snickered.

He took her derision in stride. He couldn't tell her how he'd pulled into the driveway and felt that he'd come home. Penelope's presence had made it clear what a contrast this life was with life back in New York. This was where he belonged. If not here, then he would find somewhere else, but Molly wouldn't be there. It was here that he imagined having a home and family. It was Molly he wanted them with. He was getting ahead of himself, but he could see it so clearly in the future. For now, he would spare her that vision.

He said plainly, "I've made an offer, but Liz won't accept it unless you agree."

Molly smiled, no doubt with relief. "Not gonna happen."

"I know. But she's given me a week to convince you." Zach gave Molly some time to let that settle.

She spoke slowly, as if to a very young child. "It's. Not. Happening." She glanced over at the bar. "I think I'll take Hal up on that offer."

Of all the things she had said, that comment bothered him most. "I'll drive you home." This whole talk had gone wrong in so many ways. Molly got up, and Zach pulled out a couple of twenties and left them on the table.

Molly glanced down. "We're not in Manhattan."

"It's Christmas." He left the bills where they were and followed her out.

As he pulled into the long driveway that led to the Christmas Tree Inn, Zach was struck by its contrast with the bar they'd just come from. Strings of lights stretched from tree to tree along the perimeter and rows of trees in front of the tree farm. The inn was similarly lit with a warm glow emanating from every window. The snow's surface reflected the pale light from the moon, while warm splotches of color from the evergreen trees in the yard cast a holiday sheen on the inn. In the distance, shadows of the mountains framed the whole scene. It was beautiful but empty for Zach, like a leftover Christmas card to be boxed up with no meaning or purpose until the next year.

He parked, and Molly wasted no time getting out. Zach hopped down and met her as she rounded the back of the truck.

"Go home, Zach." She kept walking.

"No." He leaned against the back bumper and folded his arms.

Molly stopped and turned.

Zach made no effort to leave, follow her, or explain his intentions. This was the moment he knew he'd lost his mind.

"What?" She stared as though she knew it, too.

But by then, he'd accepted his fate. "Your mother gave me till the new year."

It was an evening of revelations. Not only did he

know how deeply Molly resented—if not hated—him, but he also knew without any doubt that he loved her.

She stared in disbelief, which made sense because he couldn't believe it either. Within days he would have to convince her to approve of his buying the farm.

"Suit yourself." She marched to the inn.

FOURTEEN

MOLLY TRIED but did not manage to completely avoid Zach the next day. Instead, they arrived at a tacit acceptance of their forced proximity. He had never dared venture into the owner's wing she shared with her mother, so that space was safe—although he was getting awfully chummy with Will, so she worried Will might invite Zach to the kitchen for coffee. Why her mother hadn't rejected Zach's offer outright, she could not understand. Her mother seemed to have developed a soft spot for Zach.

While cleaning up after breakfast, Molly brought some dishes to the sink, where she happened to look through the window and catch sight of Zach at the farm. Will seemed to be giving him the VIP treatment, taking Zach around the farm, pointing here and there in an apparent effort to acquaint Zach with the whole operation. Will, too, seemed to be on board with the sale.

Zach could tour all he wanted, but it was Molly who would have the last word. And that word was no.

It had snowed overnight, leaving a fresh coat for the annual Christmas Eve sleigh ride. Always a festive event, it didn't happen without some preparation. Baked goods, coffee, and cocoa—not to mention plenty of wood—had to be ready at the large fire pit, where people would gather to sing Christmas carols while they waited for their turn at the sleigh. A neighboring farmer supplied horses to pull the sleigh, which was kept at the tree farm. Mounted on the sleigh were six forward-facing benches, with lap blankets for each. The event was always a holiday favorite, but with a fresh snowfall and a clear evening, tonight's would be undeniably romantic—so much so that couples sometimes returned from the sleigh ride engaged to be married.

They all worked to prepare—even Zach—and by evening, everything was ready, and the people arrived. Zach brought a tray of cocoa to a group of her mother's friends, and he lingered for a moment. They were too far away for Molly to hear what they were saying, but from the bright smiles and light laughter, he appeared to be charming the ladies. *Figures.* She rolled her eyes.

We all fall for it once. Molly inwardly grumbled as Zach walked away.

One of her mother's friends, Lydia, spied Molly and approached. *That's what I get for being distracted.* Ordinarily, she would be as chipper and chatty as they were, but she just wasn't up to her usual holiday cheer.

"Who's your friend?" There was no mistaking who Lydia was talking about.

Molly followed her eyes to Zach, who was lifting a child onto the sleigh. *Oh, come on! What next? Go ahead. Rescue a puppy, why don't you?* "Oh, that's Zach."

Lydia raised an eyebrow. "Zach."

Molly shrugged. "Yeah. He's a guest." She laughed lightly. "We can't seem to get rid of him."

Lydia leaned closer. "Why would you want to?"

Molly forced a smile.

Lydia studied Zach. "I would hang onto him."

"Yeah?" Molly looked about and planned her escape.

"Look at him."

Must I? Out of politeness, Molly looked at the object of Lydia's admiration. Zach was walking away.

Lydia said, "Nice—"

"Guy. Yeah, he is. Excuse me. I need to replenish the cookie tray."

The cookie trays were full, as was the cocoa

dispenser. Molly checked the indicator in the coffee machine.

"It's all full. I'm keeping tabs on it." Molly's heart skipped a beat as a voice sounded from behind, startling her. They'd been working together all day, but they'd managed to avoid speaking, for the most part. Now he was breaking the unspoken rules.

"Zach."

"Hi. Trays are loaded, beverage dispensers are full. There are logs on the fire. I'm keeping my eye on that, too. The sleigh will be back soon to take the last group."

"Great. It looks like everything's under control." Molly would have walked away if she weren't cornered by the L-shaped table arrangement.

"It's really nice, what you and your mother have done here."

"Thanks." She glanced about at the festive lights and decorations and at the fire pit outside, surrounded by people full of holiday cheer. They were singing and laughing, and it softened her mood. This was the moment she looked forward to every year. When the mad rush was over and everyone retreated to their homes, quiet peace settled over the farm. It was more than just pine scent and lighting. She used to think it was Christmas magic. While she was grown now and knew better, she refused to let go of the notion. The spirit of Christmas was alive at the Christmas tree farm.

One of the guests approached in search of coffee. Zach and Molly stepped aside, giving Molly an escape route. "Thanks for your help," she said and walked briskly away.

She joined her mother and Will outside for the last sleigh ride of the evening. It was a tradition that after all the guests went home, everyone left would take a sleigh ride. The team of high school and college students had all had their ride. Now they would clean everything up. They were usually finished by the time the sleigh returned from its last run. Liz called them her team of elves.

The sleigh emptied, and it was their turn. Molly, her mother, and Will would now take their annual ride. And apparently, so would Zach.

They walked over to the sleigh, and Molly stepped aside and signaled for her mother to sit with Will. The new seating arrangement was a sign of Molly's approval. Judging by the warmth in her mother's expression, Liz saw it as such, too. Molly settled into her seat, feeling content. The evening had been a success. She got wistful thinking how, this time next year, she would just be a guest from next door. She spread a blanket over her lap and leaned back with a sigh. As if a switch had been flipped, she finally felt the joy of the season. It had been a rough couple of weeks, but that was behind her. It was Christmastime, and the evening was perfect at last.

Then Zach hopped into the sleigh. Despite having ten other seats he could have chosen, he sat beside Molly.

She took in a sharp breath, but Zach put a finger to his lips to shush her. "Listen." The only sounds were the horse hooves and the scrape of the sleigh's runners on the snow-covered road. "This is amazing! I've never done this before."

That caught Molly off guard. "A sleigh ride? Never?"

"Nope." He grinned. "It's so quiet."

Molly caught herself smiling. *Let's keep it that way.* She turned away and took in the scene. She'd been lucky to grow up in a picture-perfect setting like this. She realized no one else was talking either. She glanced at Zach.

She blamed the sleigh and the moonlight for what happened next. He was looking at her as though he could see through to her soul, and she caught a glimpse of his. She had used every defense that she had to keep him from getting to her, but it all had dissolved, leaving nothing but two people looking at one another. It was honest. And terrifying.

His arm, stretched casually over the back of the

wooden bench, was mere inches from her shoulder. *Did he put it there on purpose?* It looked so natural, so comfortable that it might have landed there with no thought. Yet Molly was so aware of him that it wouldn't have surprised her if electricity had arced from his hand to her shoulder.

But he never touched her. He didn't try to kiss her. He did nothing until, by the time they arrived back at the farm, her heart ached so much for him that she was overwhelmed by an urge to take matters—and his face —into her hands and kiss him.

She hadn't yet, but she was weakening. The sleigh stopped, and Molly threw the blanket aside and got out. "Gotta go! Too much coffee!" She rushed to the inn. *What a lovely parting Christmas thought, Molly.*

FIFTEEN

MOLLY CAME out to the kitchen on Christmas morning and shuffled through her regular coffee routine. She hadn't slept well. In fact, all night she'd awoken with visions—not of sugarplums but of Zach and the kiss they might have had, which was infuriating, since she'd made up her mind not to fall prey to his magnetism. But Christmas was no time for logic. She must have tossed that into the bonfire before climbing into the sleigh—and nearly onto Zach, at least in her mind. Hence the dreams. But she hadn't acted on them, so good for her. She was fine. But those dreams were not helping.

IN THE FIRST DREAM, she'd looked at his hand on the back of the bench, then she'd looked up at him. Peering into her eyes, he said, "Your gaze moves me. Deeply." Then he lowered his face to hers, and their lips nearly touched. A deer crossed the road, and the horses both reared. The sleigh lurched then tipped to its side, nearly toppling over, and landed upright with such a jarring impact that she bumped against the bench in front of her, and her front teeth fell out. True to form, Zach would not be deterred. He touched Molly's chin and tilted her face up to his, and she smiled, looking like miserable Fantine after a dental visit. He took one look at her toothless smile and leapt from the sleigh.

Molly sat up in bed, drank some water, then turned and pulled the covers up to her chin and went back to sleep.

THEY WERE RIDING ALONG in the sleigh, and moonlight brushed her glistening hair. Molly looked at her hair, and it looked really good. She ran her fingers through the long, silky strands and tossed them over her shoulder to be caught by the wind. Emotion overwhelmed her, and tears pooled in her eyes. *I am having a really great hair day!* Zach touched her shoulder. Oh yeah. Zach was there. He looked really good, too. He ran his fingers through her hair then held a handful to his lips and breathed in. A lot. He was really into her hair. Maybe a little too much. Then he turned into the barber who cut Marty South's hair in Thomas Hardy's *The Woodlanders*, and he seemed to be under the impression that they had a similar deal.

He lifted a huge pair of sheep shears and said, "Not to worry. I'll love you no matter how bad your hair looks!"

"Thanks?"

Molly bolted upright, clutching her head.

It took her two hours and an audiobook to get over that dream, but she finally drifted to sleep.

Not long after, a voice called out from the mist. "Molly Fosterrr..."

"Huh?" She flopped over and covered her ears with her pillow.

"Molly Fosterrr..."

She grunted. "Leave me alone."

"I am—"

She sat up. "Yeah, I get it. You're the ghost of whatever. Let's just cut to the chase."

"Molly."

Through the mist, there floated an apparition

whose filmy presence hovered at the foot of her bed. "Oh, c'mon, Zach! What is your problem?"

While she waited for an answer, she took note of his robe. It was a Henry VIII number, which he didn't really need with those broad shoulders of his. Still, he looked kind of hot in his Tudor attire, not that she would ever tell him.

He looked quizzically at her. "Why not?"

"Because... Wait, I did not say that out loud."

He looked a little too pleased. "No, but hey. It's your dream. If you want me to read your mind, then who am I to complain?"

"But I don't!"

"Whatever." He shrugged, sauntered across the room, and looked absently out the window.

Crap. The last thing I need is for him to know that I love him.

"Aha!" He leapt across the room like a gymnast and stuck the landing right next to her bed. He fell to his knees beside her and clutched her hand. "I knew it!"

"No, you didn't," she protested. "I've been very careful to avoid letting you see how I felt."

"Why? You know how I feel."

"And if you can read minds, then you know how I feel. I don't trust you."

He rolled his eyes while suppressing a laugh. "Trust?" He slipped his hand under her head, and for some reason that defied the neckline circumference, her sleep T-shirt slipped off her shoulders. He drew her close, and even in dreams, she was only human. So she let him gaze deeply into her eyes, and she might have gazed back. "Who needs trust when I can kiss you like this?"

He put his lips on hers, and dang, if he didn't have a point. *He can really kiss!*

"Thank you," he said cheerily, reading her thoughts. Then he went back to kissing the common sense out of her.

Molly tossed her head side to side, muttering, "No! I don't want to wake up!"

But she did.

HER MOTHER's footsteps padded down the hall to the kitchen. "Merry Christmas!"

They hugged, and Molly wished her the same. They drank coffee and indulged in pastries while they waited for Will to arrive, then the morning flew past in a flurry of opening wrapped boxes and gift bags.

The meal prep began, and Molly and Liz whipped up their annual favorites.

"Hey, Will, if you're gonna be part of this family, you'll have to pull your weight." Molly held out a peeler and handed him a sack of potatoes, and he got to work.

As a rule, the Christmas Tree Inn served continental breakfast and left guests on their own for the rest of the day. But they had a collection of regulars to whom Liz offered an unadvertised holiday package that included her homemade Christmas dinner. They all knew each other so well it was hardly different from anyone else's family dinner. Except for one thing. *Where is Zach?*

Dinner was almost ready and still no Zach. He was avoiding her. She didn't know what else it could be. Filled with Christmas generosity, she decided the least she could do was smooth over the tension between them for the day. So she ducked into the hallway and texted Zach. "Can we talk? I'm downstairs."

Zach texted her back. "I'm in upstate New York."

Molly: What?

Zach: I'M IN UPSTATE NEW YORK! ;)

Molly: Very funny. What's there?

Zach: Home.

Molly: Oh. I didn't know that.

Zach: Yeah.

Molly: Sorry to bother you when you're with your family.

Zach: No problem. What's up?

Molly: Oh, nothing. Just Merry Christmas.

Zach: Thanks! Same to you!

As SHE AND her mother laid out the buffet, Molly said, "Zach's gone."

Liz glanced at her daughter. "I know."

"Why didn't you tell me?"

She stopped and turned to Molly. "Oh, sorry. I assumed he told you."

"No." Molly frowned for a moment then walked to the kitchen.

By late afternoon, when the holiday meal was finished and the dishes were done, everyone sat in contented conversation by the fireplace or dozing in front of a holiday movie on TV. Refusing to call it "a nap," Molly slipped away to her room for some "quiet time." She was tired, which reminded her of the reason. She had spent the night tormented by dreams of Zach.

Exhausted, Molly lay down on her bed—a risky move, given her Christmas Eve dreams, although she wouldn't mind a rerun of that last one, the Ghost of Kiss Me Now.

Zach and dreams of him aside, she'd had a wonderful Christmas, so it all had worked out. Zach was gone, so she'd gotten her way. That was easy.

So why do I miss him?

SIXTEEN

In some ways, the day after Christmas was Molly's favorite. The frenzy of Christmas was over—the decorating, the shopping, the wrapping, and the cooking. But the magic of Christmas still hung in the air. After a day indoors, everyone was ready to explore the outdoors or go into the village—including her mother and Will. The fridge was full of amazing leftovers, and the inn was quiet. Molly sipped her coffee and looked out at the clear, sunny day and decided to go for a walk. Later on, she would come home to indulge in a Christmas movie, more coffee, or whatever she felt like. The inn and the day were her own.

Then a black sports car pulled into the driveway and changed everything. *I thought he sold it. Did the sale fall through?* Or maybe he decided farm life wasn't for him, and he backed out of the truck deal and got his car back. Too bad Liz wasn't here, but Molly would gladly relay the good news.

The car door opened, but it wasn't Zach who got out. *Carson Attwell? What is he doing here?* He seemed like a nice enough guy. They'd gotten on well in the job interview, but learning that Zach had arranged it left Molly feeling uncomfortable. He was Zach's friend, not hers. All of which brought her back to her original question. *Why is he here?* There was a downside to owning an inn. Anyone could show up and invade the space.

"Carson Attwell! Hello!"

"Molly. Good to see you again." They shook hands, then he went to the trunk and pulled out a small bag.

Molly blamed the holiday activities for her not having kept up to date with guest reservations. He looked like he was going to stay. Following his lead, she smiled and walked inside with him. Kicking into autopilot, she found his reservation. Apparently there had been a last-minute cancellation, and he had lucked into a vacancy. She checked him in and gave him his key. He still hadn't explained why he was here. In fact, he'd been quite evasive. But this was an inn, not an interrogation room, so she had to accept his presence with or without a good reason for it.

She was directing him to his room when the front

door opened and Zach walked in. While the two men greeted one another amiably and shared driving times and traffic stories, Molly took a look at the reservations again. Zach had never checked out. He was still booked until New Year's Day. She looked up, confused.

"Everything okay, Molly?" Zach asked.

Zach and Carson were staring at her.

"Yeah, fine. I just thought... Didn't you say you were in Upstate New York?"

Zach smiled amiably. "Yesterday. And now I'm here."

Molly managed to nod as though this were no more important than the weather.

Carson broke the silence. "Zach has said so much about this place that I had to come up here and see for myself. And I always welcome the chance to spend time with Zach. He's a great guy! But you knew that."

Molly stared for a moment. "Yes. Great guy." She looked from Carson to Zach. Even Zach looked a little uncomfortable. "Well. I'll let you two great guys get caught up. Enjoy your stay at the Christmas Tree Inn."

The two men turned toward the stairs, and when Carson started to carry his bag to his room, Molly wasted no time heading to the kitchen. She hoped her heart rate, not to mention her heart in general, would go back to normal.

Molly regained her composure and was at the desk

when Will and Liz returned. They stood by the desk and were chatting with Molly when Zach and Carson came downstairs in their jackets.

Once the greetings were dispensed with, Carson said, "We were just on our way out for lunch. Anyone care to join us?" He looked straight at Molly.

"We just came back from lunch," offered Will. All eyes turned to Molly.

She froze for a moment then frowned. "I can't. I have desk duty." *Phew.*

Liz said, "We can cover the desk. Go ahead."

Thanks, Mom. Then a brilliant thought came to her. With deep disappointment, Molly said, "But three people won't fit in that little car." *Too bad.*

"But we'll fit in the truck."

Thanks, Carson. So maybe she hadn't thought through her brilliant excuse. Of course Zach had come separately. In a vehicle. His.

"Great. I guess I'll go get my jacket and purse." Molly went to her room and checked her hair and makeup—and she was wearing none. Gorgeous. *They're waiting, so it is what it is.*

A half hour later, the three of them walked into a hillside restaurant. If she hadn't been so uneasy, she would have been charmed by the tiny white lights and natural greenery artfully arranged in all the right places. But the charm was why she'd suggested this place. She knew it would not disappoint even these two guys from the city. They were seated at a table near the fireplace, where a crackling fire warmed the room, and the windows looked out on a stunning mountain view.

Carson, she discovered, had not mastered the art of the deal. He was doing a really hard sell on Zach. It was like having a delectable meal in a magnificent setting while watching an hour-long infomercial.

While Zach's life had its interesting moments, hearing the whole story in one sitting was getting to her. If she were Zach, she would be embarrassed. Whether he was, she couldn't tell, because she didn't dare look at him.

With little opportunity to talk, Molly gave up. She sat back and listened to Carson drone on while she sipped her cranberry mimosa.

Carson finished his story. "But that's just Zach." He leaned back and laughed.

When the laughter subsided, Molly decided that she'd had enough. She emptied her glass and set it down on the table. "Well, now all that's left is to die and wait five years."

The two men stared, clearly baffled, so Molly explained. "For sainthood. You have to be dead for five years and jump through some hoops before you can be canonized for sainthood. But it sounds like you're well on the way, Zach." She laughed, delighted with herself. She was laughing alone. She pulled out her phone, did a quick search, and scrolled. "Let's see. We've covered step one. Step two, become a servant of God. I'm sure selling real estate's close enough. Three, heroic virtue. You look like a hero, and according to Carson, you act like one, too. Four, verified miracle. I'll verify that. You got me to like you." Her amusement faded. "So, I guess you are a saint." She spied her glass, which had been refilled when she wasn't looking. She reached for it, but Zach intercepted her hand, lowered it to the table, and held it in his.

Molly stared at their hands. "You have nice hands."

Zach signaled to the waiter and settled the check while Carson beckoned the busboy and asked him to take Molly's mimosa.

Zach finished signing the check. "Time to go."

"But I like it here."

"So do I." He and Carson exchanged looks, and Zach took Molly's hand and steadied her while she stood and looked at him with open, unguarded eyes. "And I like you."

"I like you, too." Zach pivoted her in the direction of the door.

"I like you, too, Carson, as a friend. But I like Zach a lot more."

Carson raised an eyebrow, then they maneuvered

their way through a labyrinth of occupied tables and chairs until they arrived at the door. Zach put his arm about Molly's waist and guided her to the truck. While Zach pulled out his keys, Carson opened the door. Molly leaned into Zach's chest and breathed in, then she murmured, "You smell so good. I could love you, but I could never trust you."

ZACH GRASPED her wrists and gently removed them. "In you go."

She climbed into the truck, and Carson hopped into the back seat.

As they pulled into the inn's long driveway, Molly yawned. "I need a nap."

Zach nodded and caught Carson's smile in the rearview mirror. "Sounds like a good idea."

She said, "Yeah, but then I'll dream of you again." Her eyes widened as she leaned toward him. "You would not believe my Christmas Eve dream. You were Henry the Eighth." She poked her finger at his chest. "You, sir, look amazing in tights. And don't get me started on that kiss." She turned back to Carson. "Tudors! Who knew? There's more to them than just wattle and daub."

Zach and Carson each took a side and guided

Molly to the front door. Zach muttered, "This is going to be my fault."

Carson nodded. "Probably."

"I don't remember them filling her glass all that much."

Carson looked guilty. "Must have been while I was talking."

"Yeah. About that."

"Too much?"

Zach nodded. "Yup."

"Sorry."

Zach opened the door. There was no sign of Liz, but Will sat by the fire, reading. He looked up, caught sight of Molly, and lifted an eyebrow. "How was brunch?"

Molly clung to Zach. "I think I need a nap."

Zach looked at Will. "We'll just walk her to her room."

Will returned to his book. "Stop by on your way out."

They put Molly to bed and went to face Will. Zach launched into his defense. "Carson and I were talking, and Molly was drinking mimosas. I guess they refilled her glass a few too many times."

"Have a seat." He turned to Carson. "Would you excuse us for a minute?"

"Uh, sure. I'll go wait in the car."

Zach pulled out his keys and gave them to Carson. They exchanged intense looks with expressionless faces, then Carson quietly left.

Will set down his book. "That's not like Molly."

Zach said, "Those mimosas can go to your head."

Will narrowed his eyes and leaned back, giving the appearance of being relaxed, which for some reason intimidated Zach even more. "I've known Molly all her life. Her father was my best friend. So I'm going to say what I think he would say if he were here."

This was not going to be good.

"Don't hurt her."

Zach opened his mouth to protest. That was the last thing he wanted to do. He was falling in love, but he wasn't ready to broadcast that yet.

Will rested his elbow on the arm of his chair and leaned closer and quietly said, "If you hurt her, there will be consequences."

Will's direct gaze had the power to blacken an eye with its impact.

"Okay."

Zach climbed into the truck and leaned his head back on the headrest. "Oh, man. I feel like I'm sixteen on prom night but worse."

Carson gave his friend an understanding look. "What did he say?"

"If I hurt her, there will be consequences." Zach shut his eyes and exhaled.

Carson squinted. "That's it? Consequences?" He waved his fingers. "Whoooo. What's he gonna do, ground you?"

Not at all amused, Zach turned his head toward him. "It's not what he said. It's how he said it."

Carson stopped laughing and waited, but Zach was in no mood to explain. So he started the truck and drove off while he tried to block out the image of Will shoving him through the Christmas tree baler.

About a mile down the road, Zach said, "Wait, where are we going? We've got rooms at the inn."

Carson stared straight ahead. "Oh yeah. Good point."

MOLLY HELD the phone with one hand and her coffee mug with the other. "I think I told him I love him. No. What I said was that I *could* love him. That's totally different. Isn't it? Dakota?"

"Oh, absolutely. Not really."

Molly rested her forehead on her hand. "I know. And it gets worse."

"Hardly seems possible," Dakota said dryly.

"I told him he looked good in tights."

"I'll bet he does. No point in lying. When did you see him in tights, by the way?"

Molly shook her head. "Oh, I had this dream... Never mind."

"So, Moll. When did you take up day drinking as a hobby? I mean, don't get me wrong. It sounds more fun than golf, but it's not really your style."

"Yeah. I didn't mean to. But I was so bored. Carson just went on and on about Zach. Not that I don't find Zach an interesting topic, but storytelling isn't exactly Carson's strong suit. So, I don't know. The staff kept refilling my glass. I was thirsty, and those cranberry mimosas are good! And so, well, you know."

"I do."

Molly groaned. "I can never see them again."

Dakota laughed. "Ha! We'll fix that. Don't worry."

"No, thank you."

"Let's back up and revisit this love you spoke of."

"Ugh. I'm not going to repeat it." Molly was beginning to think that she'd made a mistake. *Another coffee and a bracing walk—that's all I need. That and a good hour of self-loathing.*

"When you shouted your love from the rooftop, what did he do?"

"I don't know. I lost track of what he was doing."

Molly ran her fingers through her hair. "By that point, everything was a bit blurry."

Dakota chuckled. "Yeah, been there. So maybe I'm looking at this from the wrong angle. He's kissed you and come back for more. And he's dragged his poor friend up here to talk him up and impress you. I think his feelings are obvious."

Molly leaned back and stared out the window. She wondered why it couldn't snow now. It would make everything look fresh and new.

"So, Molly. I've figured it out."

"Yeah?"

"You're in love."

"Oh, come on, Dakota!" Molly got up and paced. "It's the drink. People say things."

Dakota said quietly, "Things that are true."

That was not Dakota's kidding voice. Worse than that, she was right.

"Molly?"

"Yes?"

"Am I right? I mean, I know I am, but I'm waiting for you to admit it."

Molly exhaled. "I can't love him. Well, that's not true. I can, obviously. But I don't want to."

Dakota said, "I wish we were having this conversation in person."

Molly's eyes filled with tears. "So you could give me a hug?"

"Actually, this is the part in the old movies where the woman is in hysterics and someone has to slap her, because that's so conducive to clear thinking. They didn't really get women back then. Yeah, you're right. A hug would be better."

Molly laughed in spite of herself.

"So, Moll, face it. You're in love."

"I don't want to be."

"I know. But love doesn't always give us a choice. Look at me and Tom Hardy. We're from two different worlds, Hollywood and Vermont. But the heart wants what the heart wants. And apparently, my heart's not very needy, so an imaginary boyfriend will do."

"There must be someone a little more local."

"You know, seriously, I'm pretty happy alone. Don't get me wrong. If Tom Hardy came to his senses, then fine. But my happiness doesn't depend on him."

"That sounds so smart. Maybe I've got it all wrong."

"No! No, that's not what I meant. You, my friend, are in love. He's in love. That's a game changer."

"I don't know."

"So you say, but I think you do."

"Yeah?"

"Think about it. Time's up for this session. Let's pick up here tomorrow."

"What's tomorrow?"

"I'm coming over to knock your heads together. The Three Stooges were ground-breaking visionaries."

Molly laughed. "Okay. Tomorrow. Text me in the morning."

"Will do."

SEVENTEEN

MOLLY HID out in her room until Zach and Carson went skiing. They didn't come in until late. Molly heard them from the kitchen and made a hasty exit to her room.

But a new day had dawned, which was supposed to signal a new beginning. She didn't feel it, but she knew she couldn't put it off any longer. She needed to face him today. The longer she waited, the worse she would feel when she and Zach ran into each other, which they would do before long. The best thing would be to meet in a controlled environment. If all went well, by tomorrow, they would have a good laugh about it.

Molly took a deep breath and texted Zach. "Can we talk?" She sent it and put her hand to her pounding chest.

Zach: Sure. When?

Molly: Uh...I don't know.

Zach: Now?

Molly: Okay.

Zach: Where?

Molly: I just realized that there's no place private here.

Zach: Not that bar. Please.

Molly: Meet me downstairs.

She couldn't have taken more than two seconds to check her hair and face in the mirror before she left her room, but he was there waiting at the foot of the stairs. She decided to act as if everything were normal until they got to their destination. "I should have asked you to bring your keys."

He pulled them from his pocket.

"Good. I thought of a place. Talking's impossible here, and everyone's off for the week and roaming around town. So I thought of a place."

"Good. Let's go."

Molly directed him along a narrow road that wound its way through enormous, strewn boulders. When they reached the top, Zach pulled into a small parking area beside the road. They got out of the truck, and Molly led Zach along a path to a clearing that revealed a valley filled with fenced farmland.

Zach took in the view. "It's breathtaking."

Molly almost forgot to feel awkward. "I know. I

don't ever get tired of it."

He nodded, and they stood in companionable silence.

Molly didn't know how to start, so she blurted it out. "I am so sorry."

His smile put her at ease. "You said some things. Do you remember?"

For a split second, she thought about lying, but she'd never been good at it. "Yes. And I'm really sorry."

He turned to face her. "I was hoping you meant it."

She took a breath and exhaled. "I know that I said I could love you. But I'm not ready for that."

Disappointment filled his eyes, and that tugged at her heart.

He looked out to the distance. "If we hadn't met like we did, would that have changed anything?"

She knew the answer but was reluctant to say it. "Yes."

"Fair enough. But would you think about something for me?"

"Okay."

"Think about yesterday."

"I'd rather not."

"It's okay. It doesn't change how I feel about you. Yesterday was a glitch. A slight imperfection. It proves that you're human."

"That's a positive spin." *Doesn't really make me*

feel better, but what an excellent try.

He heaved a sigh. "I'm human, too. And I make mistakes. I just wish you'd forgive me for that."

"I do. But that doesn't mean you should buy the Christmas tree farm."

"Right. The farm." Zach looked away.

"Anyway, I just wanted to tell you I'm sorry for yesterday." Molly turned and led the way back to the truck.

Zach stared for a moment then followed. When they reached the truck, Molly said, "Maybe if things were different, if we had more time... no pressure..."

"Three days. That's what we've got." He looked sideways at her.

"For the farm. Not for me."

They climbed into the truck, and Zach started the engine but made no move to leave. He studied her for a moment then looked away. "It's funny. I look at the Christmas tree farm, and I could see us, what could be us, there. I see my past, growing up on a farm, dovetailing with what I've become. And now, I see you, and I don't want to lose you." He searched her eyes. "Am I delusional? Have I misread the signals?"

For that, she blamed herself. "No. But there's more to it than feelings. There are other factors involved."

"Maybe. In my experience, people can talk themselves in or out of anything. Those other factors can be used to argue either way. And the higher the stakes, the more complications there are, and more ways to construe them. But those are just distractions. At some point, you have to strip all that stuff away and look at the core issue. For me, that issue is you. The farm is just a means to that end."

"How Machiavellian of you."

"Wow. That was a hugely negative spin on what, from my point of view, was an embarrassing declaration of love."

How did I completely miss that? Was I trying so hard to protect myself that I had no clue about his feelings?

Zach said, "Let me rephrase that. The farm would make us both happy, and being together on the farm would be perfect."

Molly wondered why everything felt so forced, and the answer came to her. "It's the farm. If it weren't for that, it would just be about us. We could get to know each other with no deadline or expectations."

Zach nodded. "That's my fault. I saw a life that I wanted, and I did what I always do. I went for it."

"And put pressure on me to decide." It looked so easy for him to make an enormous decision with no guarantee about the future.

Zach studied her. "Did I? I guess I did. But I didn't see a way around it."

"I do. Leave the farm out of it. Otherwise, I feel like a real estate transaction." There. She'd said it. She felt relieved.

"I could. But here's how that plays out. I don't buy the farm. I go back to my business. We phone, text, and video chat. We touch base every day. Then it's every few days, weeks, and finally months. Left alone, at a distance, what we have becomes less and less real. We get busy, and in time, we lose touch."

Like a breakup for cowards. "We don't know that." But it made too much sense to dismiss it.

He smiled cynically.

Frustration mounted within her. "We don't know anything. We just met, and I'm supposed to be sure of what takes people months to know."

"Thank your mother for that. She's the one who gave me a week."

"Oh, that's convenient. Blame my mother." She turned toward the window.

"I'm not blaming anyone. It's just bad timing. But you can't let things like timing control you. You either let life happen to you, or you can make the life you want happen."

"Where did you get that, from your inspirational desk calendar?" She could see why he was so good at sales. The man would not give up.

"No, I learned it the hard way."

Molly searched his eyes. "I'm glad that works for you. But while you're over there making life happen, I'm over here feeling backed into a corner and forced into a decision I'm not ready for."

His expression softened. "I don't want you to feel that way."

"Then leave me alone or just give me some time." Even to Molly's ears, that sounded harsh.

Apparently, he agreed, since he abruptly pulled onto the road and headed to the inn. Neither spoke, but they both appeared calmer by the time they pulled in and parked. Calm or in shock.

Without a word, Zach got out and went around to her side. She hadn't been waiting for that. Instead, she felt stuck, unable to move. But he opened the door to their unpleasant reality. Molly stared at the farm for a moment. She saw her father and mother, and Will, and all that had happened over the past several years. All Zach saw was her. It even felt good, in a sense, but there were too many other things getting in the way.

They walked together and stopped at the inn's entrance. Molly looked into Zach's eyes. "I'm sorry. All I wanted was to apologize for my condition at brunch."

His expression softened, and he opened his arms. That simple gesture seemed to push aside all of what he called "distractions," and she sank into his embrace. *What am I doing? This is not helping.*

Zach said, "We'll figure it out."

Her confusion began to lift like a morning fog. She tried to memorize the feel of his arms around her, then she lifted her face to his.

"Part of me wants what you want. But I'm not ready, for this or the farm. I honestly wish I could be." She turned and headed inside to her room.

CARSON AND DAKOTA looked up from their card game as Molly rushed past, clearly upset.

Dakota dropped her cards and stood up. "Molly?"

"Not now." She went to her room.

Then Zach burst through the door and headed up the stairs.

"Zach?" Dakota turned to Carson. "Well, we can't just do nothing." She headed for Molly's room.

Zach's door was open, so Carson stepped inside. Zach had half of his clothing wadded and shoved into his suitcase and was well on the way to finishing the task.

Carson leaned on the door frame. "You have to understand, I'm an archivist. We're not people people. So you're going to have to help me out here. What's going on?"

Zach looked up. "I'm leaving."

Carson eyed the suitcase and said softly, "Yes. I gathered as much."

"It's over." Zach finished packing and paused long enough to say, "We can talk back in New York, when I don't feel like... a hot steamy pile of frigging feelings."

Carson nodded, confused.

With a gruff goodbye, Zach wasted no time leaving. By the time Carson reached the foot of the stairs, he heard Zach's truck driving down the long driveway.

MOLLY DABBED her red eyes while her mother looked on. Molly had already gone over everything with Dakota and mercifully sent her on her way. There was nothing Dakota or anyone else could do. Her mother arrived as Dakota was leaving. The two spoke in hushed tones, then her mother knocked on her door.

"Come in." Molly looked at her mother. "He's gone. I just couldn't make a decision like that in a week."

Liz sat on the edge of Molly's bed. "I'm so sorry. I feel responsible."

"Why?"

"The farm. If I didn't need the proceeds to fund my retirement, I could have waited to sell."

"And then what would Zach have done? He wouldn't have just hung around here, waiting for me to figure out what I want to do when I grow up. Look at him. The guy needs a project, his work or the farm."

Liz nodded sympathetically.

Molly shook her head. "It was this one moment in time where our lives could have converged. It was almost perfect." Molly sighed. "Except it was too soon."

Liz said, "It's pretty amazing that he was willing to leave everything behind and begin a new life."

"It's not like it was all for me. He was ready for a change. He just didn't realize it until he came here and saw the life that he wanted. I have no doubt he'll find a farm somewhere."

"You don't think that it might have been more about you?"

Molly shrugged. "He'll find his way to the life that he wants. But I won't be in it."

Liz rubbed Molly's shoulder the way she used to when she was a girl, then she got a wastebasket and held it out.

Molly loaded at least two dozen used tissue wads into the receptacle and tried to laugh. "I think I've dehydrated myself." She was quiet for a few moments. "Did I do the right thing? Part of me wanted to do it without thinking. Be with him and figure the rest out later. You know? But I couldn't help feeling like I'd be jumping off a cliff. It would feel great at first, like flying. But then I would land, and it wouldn't be pretty."

"That's an awfully harsh analogy, Molly." Liz smiled gently.

Molly tried to smile back. "It was scary."

"It's a lot to take on all at once."

Molly leaned her head back against the headboard and hugged her knees to her chest. "I think it was for him, too, but he's more of a risk taker. I just couldn't be sure it would be the right thing. How did you know with Daddy?"

Liz smiled and appeared to recall earlier days. "It's a small village. Your father and I practically grew up together. Same classes, same school, same friends. It was like we'd always known it would happen. By the time we were old enough to consider being together, we knew we'd be together forever. But forever didn't turn out to be as long as we thought it would." Liz shut her eyes and tamped down a surge of emotion.

Sounds from the kitchen brought Molly back to the present. It was Will making coffee. "And then there's Will. He was Garrett's best friend."

Molly stared straight ahead with a hopeless expression. "Years from now, I don't want to look back on this and know this was the point where I ruined my life. How do you know when it's right? Which direction to take?"

"I don't think one way is right and the other is wrong. They're just different. You choose, and then that's your life." She put her hand on Molly's. "And sometimes life throws surprises at you. Some good, some bad."

Still troubled, Molly said, "But there's got to be a way to know what the right answer is."

"Life isn't a multiple-choice test where you bubble in an answer and find out if it's right."

"Well, it should be. It should come with directions or at least a warning label." Molly almost smiled.

Liz nodded. "Some people say you just know. But I think those people are lucky. I was. Even so, no one ever really knows. You just have to believe in each other enough to risk it."

Molly didn't feel better, but at least she felt calmer.

Liz gave her daughter a hug. "Things have a way of working out."

"But do they really, Mom?"

Liz gave her a confident nod. "Yes. Because if they don't, then we'll just have to make them work out. In the meantime, I've got a pint of ice cream in the fridge with our names on it." She tugged Molly by the hand. "Come on."

EIGHTEEN

Rain drizzled down the wall of windows in Zach's high-rise apartment as he sat staring at the city lights blurred by the raindrops. His phone dinged to signal an incoming message.

Carson: Wanna talk?

Zach: About what?

Carson: About how I'm downstairs?

The intercom by his apartment door rang. Zach answered it. "Send him up."

A minute later, Zach opened the door.

"So, what's new?" Carson asked.

"Oh, nothing."

"Yeah, that's what I figured."

"Sit down. I'll get you a beer." Zach went to the fridge and returned with Carson's favorite craft beer.

"How did you know?"

Zach smirked. "Because it's my favorite beer, and I told you about it."

Carson said, "So, what's new? Oh yeah, your dramatic exit. I think you hurt Vermont's feelings."

Zach shook his head. "It was just..." He shrugged. "A staggering failure."

Carson smiled. "It happens."

Zach leaned back in his black leather sofa. "I didn't know love could hit you like that, like a natural disaster you never saw coming."

"Maybe don't put it that way when you're talking with Molly," Carson said wryly.

"Oh, I'm sure she's on the same page. It's a moot point, anyway, since we won't be talking again."

"Which brings me to the reason for this little visit. What happened?"

"Told you. Failure."

"Would you care to elaborate?"

Zach heaved a weary sigh. "I didn't know till I spent some time there, but I missed farm life. It's simple. You work hard. Things grow. And the only bullshit you have to deal with is from actual bulls."

Carson wrinkled his nose. "Smells worse, though."

"Country air. It's good for the soul."

"Wow. Don't tell me you keep a pair of overalls next to your tailor-made suits."

"I would. If she'd have me."

"Oh. Ow."

"It was like life's little joke. All the right things were there in front of me, all mixed up in the wrong order. And I couldn't seem to straighten it out. What are the odds?"

Carson looked out the window. "Actually, some of us don't even get that far, so..."

"Something's been missing for a long time. Then there I was on a farm. It was perfect and just what I needed. And Molly was even more perfect. But the timing was not."

Carson rubbed his chin as if in thought. "Well, I'd have definitely dumped Penelope sooner, regardless of anything else. What did you ever see in her?"

Zach hated to admit it. "She was hot."

"Yeah, but what did you talk about?"

"She did most of the talking." Zach caught Carson's eye and couldn't help smiling. "Don't look at me like that. You've made a few choices yourself. Let's go through a scrapbook of your past relationships. Shall we?"

Carson lifted his hands in surrender. "Point taken. Let's get back to your problems. They're more fun."

Zach's mirth was short-lived. "It's weird, though. If Penelope hadn't booked us a week at the inn, I would never have met Molly."

Carson peered at Zach. "Wow. She's like a matchmaker savant."

"With a cruel sense of humor." Zach took a swig of beer. "I could have loved Molly wherever she was. But right there on that farm, it felt right."

Carson shook his head. "I'm still getting my head wrapped around the idea of you as a farmer, but other than that, I can see it."

"Too bad Molly couldn't."

LIZ AND WILL went inside the mudroom and stomped the snow from their boots. Liz hung her jacket on a peg. "I will not miss the cold or the snow, except at Christmas."

"We'll come up here for the holidays, then we'll go back before the snow gets dirty." Will followed Liz to the fireplace, and they settled there with their books.

Liz looked up from her book and stared into the fire. "Even though they got off to a rough start, I think Zach would have been good for Molly."

Without looking up from his book, Will said, "Ayup."

"Maybe if she hadn't felt pressured. You know?"

"Ayup."

Liz shook her head. "I feel responsible for that.

Putting the farm up for sale just made everything worse."

Will looked up from his book. "Life doesn't come gift wrapped."

"I know. She does, too. But ever since Garrett died, Molly has gone out of her way to avoid change and risk. Then along comes Zach, and he's all that and more." Her eyes lit with new understanding. "Zach was a surprise she wasn't ready for. Love is a force, and she couldn't control it."

Will looked up and gazed at her.

"But my selling the farm was the last straw. It turned her whole world upside down."

Will smiled. "You turned my world upside down. I didn't mind it a bit."

Liz looked at Will, one of life's surprises. If only Zach could be Molly's Will—someone there for her, waiting for when she woke up and realized he'd been there all along, and she loved him.

Then it came to her. "She needs Zach here, waiting for her to wake up."

Will looked confused. "I didn't know she was asleep."

Liz smiled. "In a way, yes, she is. But I think I can fix it!"

"Fix what? What's broken?"

Liz stood up. "Come on. We've got things to do. I'll explain as we go."

THE DAY before New Year's Eve brought the inn back to life from the quiet days after Christmas. Garrett had begun the tradition of having a New Year's Eve party for everyone who had ever worked at the farm. Over the years, it had grown to include friends and families of friends. With Liz and Will retiring and moving down south, this might be the last one.

Liz opened the kitchen door to Dakota. "I am so glad you're here. She spent all day yesterday in her pajamas and wouldn't leave her room."

Dakota said, "What I wouldn't give for a day off like that." She laughed but was suddenly serious. "But not brokenhearted."

Liz looked intently at Dakota. "You've got to get her out of this funk before tomorrow. She can't miss the New Year's Eve party."

Dakota straightened her posture and saluted. "I'm on it."

Liz smiled and sent Dakota down the hall to Molly's room then returned to her New Year's Eve party preparations.

Dakota heard a faint "Come in."

"Hey, Moll! Nice pajamas!"

Not amused, Molly said, "Thanks."

Okay. Cheerful's not working. "So, what's going on?"

Molly looked annoyed. "You know."

Dakota considered the best way to word what she wanted to say but gave up. Tact had never been her forte. "Molly, explain something to me. The guy's crazy about you. You dump him. And now you're acting as though he dumped you."

Molly rolled her eyes. "I wish life were that simple."

So far no good. "Dakota pulled Molly's desk chair closer and sat down. "Let's unpack this."

Molly rolled her eyes.

"Keep doing that, and your eyes will get stuck."

Molly nearly smiled.

Victory! Sort of. "So you love him."

Molly looked straight at Dakota. "That just makes it worse."

"What? Loving him or admitting it?"

"Yes."

"So you love him." *That's progress.*

Molly wrinkled her face and stared at the floor.

One step back. "But you don't want him to buy the farm."

"No."

"Because...?"

Molly exhaled. "Well, I do. But I don't."

Dakota opened her mouth then closed it. She actually understood less than when she'd walked through the door.

Molly came out of her fog and leaned on her elbows. "Imagine you've got a date."

Dakota grinned. "I am liking where this is going!"

Molly smiled. "Everything's great. He's great! Then you go on the date, and it all goes terribly wrong. You don't ever want to see him again. Then he moves in next door, and you have to share a driveway. And then every day is a reminder of your failure and your overall sorry existence."

"All that from one date?" Dakota was speechless, an almost impossible state for her.

Frustration burned in Molly's eyes. "From Zach! He's the date. Never mind. My point is, there's too much at stake."

"Really?" Dakota was glad no one else could see her, because she was pretty sure her face was scrunched up like an old gum wrapper, gum included.

Molly's look of frustration subsided, and one of hopeless defeat took its place. "When my father died, I just wanted everything to stop changing. I wanted a life I could count on where I would feel safe. I vowed I would never go through that kind of upheaval again."

Dakota had no snappy comeback for that, so she was silent.

Molly's eyes shimmered. "With Zach..." She took a breath. "He's good-looking and thoughtful. He's smart, hard-working—"

Dakota acted horrified. "Ugh! I see what you mean! What a loser!"

"I could love him so much that he could hurt me."

"Hurt you? You can't mean—"

"Oh no, not like that! He would never hurt me on purpose. I know that. But if he buys the farm, I know I'll fall in love. And it will be deep. And if something goes wrong, then my heart will break."

"That sounds a bit catastrophic." Dakota's eyebrows drew together. "Or he might make you happy. What if he's the best thing that's ever happened to you, but you drove him away out of fear?"

"At least my heart would be safe."

"No, Molly. Talk about risk! So you'd give all that up—all that meaning Zach—to be safe? Refusing to love or be loved? That's no way to live."

A loud clang came from the kitchen, and Liz cried out using words Molly rarely heard from her mother.

"Sounds like your mom needs some help." Dakota

took on a sterner tone. "Molly. Are you gonna sit there in your pajamas, or are you gonna go out there and help your mother?" Guilt was her fail-safe strategy.

Molly smirked. "Let me get dressed, and I'll meet you out there."

NINETEEN

Liz stood in the middle of the barn, which was cleared out to make room for a dance floor. The heaters were running to warm up the barn for the dance. White lights were strung through the rafters. Tables were arranged around the perimeter, and the buffet table was ready for food. The deejay was finishing his sound checks, and the bartender stood behind the bar, ready to serve.

Molly joined her mother. "It looks great, Mom. You've done it again."

Liz smiled. "We've done it."

It was the end of an era, and Molly knew that must be on her mother's mind. It was on hers. As much as she'd tried to keep her life consistent, she had no control over the sale of the barn. She took in a deep breath and exhaled. But she still had the inn, and her mother would visit. Her life would not change all that much. Feelings for Zach nagged her constantly, but she had to believe she would get over him one day. In the meantime, Zach was a presence in her heart that would not stop aching.

Molly steered clear of the champagne. She didn't need to relive the mimosa incident. Always the life of the party, Dakota was getting it started. She beckoned Molly over to dance with a group of their friends, but Molly forced a bright smile and waved her off. The mood was festive as ever, and everyone was having a good time. And there was Molly in the midst of it all. She switched into autopilot and went through the motions she'd gone through for years, touching base with guests and making sure they were enjoying themselves.

As the evening went on, Molly fulfilled her social obligations, then found an out-of-the-way spot where she could be alone with her thoughts. At one point, she caught sight of her mother and Dakota. The two had their heads together, and Dakota had her scheming face on—narrow eyes, the slow nods. Molly had seen it before, and it did not bode well. But someone brushed past Molly with a quick greeting. When Molly looked back, they were gone.

The music stopped, and the deejay introduced her mother. She took center stage on the small platform in front and was handed a mic. Molly glanced at her watch. It was only eleven. This wasn't part of their usual New Year's Eve routine. *What is my mother doing?*

Liz lifted her hand to her forehead to block the bright lights, and she searched the crowd. "Molly?"

Some helpful person yelled, "Over here!" and pointed at Molly.

Thanks. Reluctant but left with no choice, Molly went to her mother but not without shooting her a sharp, questioning look.

Liz smiled as though this were something they did every day. But in all the years they had thrown this New Year's Eve party, there had never been speeches. Molly turned to her mother and opened her mouth to say something, but Liz lifted the mic and launched into an impromptu speech.

"After twenty-seven years, I am so proud to be turning over the Christmas Tree Inn to my daughter."

Molly smiled. She couldn't fault her mother for this. This was a huge step for her. It was like a retirement party, in a sense. It was also a huge step for Molly, but she preferred to take her steps out of the spotlight. But this was her mother's moment—a well-deserved one—so Molly was glad to indulge her.

Liz pulled a document from behind her back and handed it to her daughter. Molly glanced at the realtor's letterhead. Why would her mother choose this moment to have her review...? Wait a minute. This was a lease. Then the name jumped out at her. "Zach Moreton?" She looked at her mother, but Liz appeared to be ignoring her.

"The Christmas tree farm has some changes ahead. After careful thought, I have decided to lease the farm for one year to a potential buyer. If all goes well, he'll have an option to buy it. So I'd like to introduce our new tenant, and I hope you'll make him feel welcome." She stretched out her arm. "Mr. Zachary Moreton."

Molly's jaw dropped as Zach walked up to join them. He flashed a smile at the guests, glanced at Molly, and took the mic Liz handed him.

"Thank you! I look forward to getting to know all of you. But enough about me. Happy New Year!"

Liz gave a nod to the deejay, handed back the mic, and the party resumed.

While Will shook Zach's hand, Molly leaned close to her mother. "Mom, I thought I had final approval."

"Of the sale. This is only a lease. Excuse me, honey, I've got some guests to attend to." She gave Molly a hug and whispered, "Follow your heart."

That was the worst advice Molly had ever heard, from her mother or anyone else. History was full of people who had followed their hearts and made appalling decisions.

Helen of Troy caused a decade of war. Cleopatra was such a sore loser she let a snake bite her breast. Mary Shelley took the phrase "over my dead body" too literally and lost her virginity on her mother's grave. *Follow your heart.*

Liz walked away, leaving Zach and Molly together. In the corner of her eye, Molly caught sight of Dakota and Carson, who happened to be blocking her path to the exit. She doubted that was by chance. They might as well have been wide-eyed and whistling. Lucky for them, they weren't actors. Sooner or later, Molly would have to look at Zach, so she braced herself and turned to him.

Zach spoke loudly to be heard over the music. "I didn't know this would happen like this."

"But you knew it would happen?"

"What?" He bent down and turned his ear toward her.

Molly raised her voice and repeated herself.

Zach nodded. "The lease was your mother's idea. When she called me—"

"She called you?"

"I couldn't say no."

"Why not?"

As he yelled out his answer, the music suddenly stopped. "Because I love you!"

Not only did everyone hear him, but they

applauded. Zach shot a look at the deejay, who glanced down and scrambled to put on the next song.

Molly's first instinct was to panic. These last few minutes were just what she'd wanted to avoid. Now her world was upside down, and her heart felt like it was going to burst. Zach loved her? She loved him too. Why was that so hard to accept? *Follow your heart.* Her heart didn't have far to go. It was right here with Zach. To her surprise, seeing him and knowing he would be here for a year began to agree with her. Slowly, her panic subsided, making way for what was already there—love. Love was beginning to drive out the doubts that had tormented her over the past weeks.

Zach said, "There's no hurry. We can take things at your pace."

That put her at ease. She looked into his eyes, and she believed him. She trusted him.

Her mother had told her they just had to believe in each other enough to risk it, and she saw that belief in his eyes. *What's holding me back? Doubt and fear?* She couldn't let them rule her life—not when she had something stronger.

Molly said, "I think... I love you, too."

Zach took her hands in his. "Will you give me a year?"

The music stopped, and everyone was counting down the seconds until the new year.

Molly nodded. "Okay."

His face lit up. "Okay? That's a yes?"

Molly grinned. "Yes. Yes!"

Confetti drifted down on the guests as Molly threw her arms around Zach's neck. Then they kissed, and the barn doors opened to reveal fireworks outside.

Zach said, "No pressure. We've got a whole year ahead of us, with an option for life."

In that moment, as fireworks sounded and confetti floated in the air, Molly realized that no matter what the next year might bring, this felt right.

Nearby, Liz slipped her arm into Will's and walked over to Molly and Zach. "Look at them. I think it worked."

Will smiled down at Liz.

As the new year arrived, Molly kissed Zach, and he spun her around. "Happy New Year, Molly."

"I believe it will be." She felt as bright as the fireworks outside.

Carson and Dakota joined them. Dakota peered closely at Molly. "So does this mean you and Zach are together?" She exhaled, with obvious relief.

Carson smirked at Dakota. "The kissing should have been a clue. But let's make it official." He pulled the lease out of Zach's pocket. "Zach, do you take this lease to be your lawfully binding home for one year?"

Zach laughed. "I do."

"And Molly, do you think you can tolerate this guy for twelve very long months?"

"Hey," Zach protested.

Molly grinned. "I do."

Carson leaned close so only Zach would hear. "Do not hurt this woman. She's too good for you."

Zach's eyebrows drew together. "Why does everyone keep telling me that? I love her!"

"Don't tell me." Carson tilted his head toward Molly. "Tell her."

"Molly, I love you."

She said, "I love you, too."

Zach pulled Molly into his arms and kissed her.

With a satisfied grin, Carson said, "I now pronounce you tree farmer and innkeeper." He turned to Dakota. "Madam, our work here is done. Shall we?" He offered his hand, which Dakota took with a laugh, and they made their way to the middle of the dance floor.

Zach and Molly danced in what promised to be a spectacular new year at the Christmas Tree Inn and Farm.

ACKNOWLEDGMENTS

Editing by Red Adept Editing
redadeptediting.com

THANK YOU!

Thank you, reader. With so many options, I appreciate your choosing my book to read. Your opinion matters, so please consider sharing a review to help other readers.

BOOK NEWS

Would you like to know when the next book comes out? Click below to sign up for the J.L. Jarvis Journal and get book news, free books, and exclusive content delivered monthly.

news.jljarvis.com

ABOUT THE AUTHOR

J.L. Jarvis is a left-handed opera singer/teacher/lawyer who writes books. She received her undergraduate training from the University of Illinois at Urbana-Champaign and a doctorate from the University of Houston. She now lives and writes in upstate New York.

Sign up to be notified of book releases and related news:
news.jljarvis.com

Email JL at:
writer@jljarvis.com

Follow JL online at:
jljarvis.com

facebook.com/jljarvis1writer

twitter.com/JLJarvis_writer

instagram.com/jljarvis.writer

bookbub.com/authors/j-l-jarvis

pinterest.com/jljarviswriter

goodreads.com/5106618.J_L_Jarvis

amazon.com/author/B005GoM2Zo

youtube.com/UC7kodjlaG-VcSZWhuYUUl_Q

Made in United States
Orlando, FL
14 December 2022

26571856R00125